IN JUDGEMENT OF OTHERS

IN
JUDGE
MENT
OF
OTHERS

ELEANOR ANSTRUTHER

Troubador Publishing Ltd
Unit E2 Airfield Business Park,
Harrison Road, Market Harborough,
Leicestershire. LE16 7UL
Tel: 0116 2792299
Email: books@troubador.co.uk
Web: www.troubador.co.uk

ISBN 978 1836280 002

British Library Cataloguing in Publication Data.
A catalogue record for this book is available from the British Library.

Printed and bound by CPI Group (UK) Ltd, Croydon, CR0 4YY
Typeset in 11pt Minion Pro by Troubador Publishing Ltd, Leicester, UK

MIX
Paper | Supporting
responsible forestry
FSC
www.fsc.org
FSC® C013604

For my impossible friend

"It's discouraging to think how many people are shocked by honesty and how few by deceit."

Noël Coward
Blithe Spirit

1   COMMITTED

Shopping usually calmed Tessa; it gave her something to do. Through the years of her illness, the rise and fall, the itch and grab, the running until she fell, shopping had been her mainstay. It gave her comfort when she was slipping; it soothed her when she had nothing left. Before Freddy, it was clothes and candles and homeware; after he was born, the women in *JoJo Maman Bébé* knew her by name.

But he was eleven and only interested in *PlayStation* and what she needed was a new winter hat. Her baseball cap looked ridiculous. It took her no time at all to get to Chichester; it was Sunday and the roads were clear. By the time she arrived, she had it all planned out. Coffee in *Pret*, followed by a sweep of *House of Fraser*. She could have everything done by two and be in plenty of time to meet Freddy and Scott for lunch. Except in *Pret* she had a slice of cake, so nothing fitted. And she kept on looking at white jeans, even though it was autumn.

She grabbed three pairs from the rack in *River Island* and took them to the till. She could try them on at home and take them back if she didn't like them. From *Reiss* she bought two winter tops and a wrap-around cardigan. In *Ted Baker,* she saw a handbag she liked. *Oasis* was nothing but sparkly dresses, so she bought two exactly the same but in different sizes. In *LK Bennet,* she found the perfect heels, and as she passed the window of *Warehouse,* a mac caught her eye. It was almost the same as the one she had on, only cleaner, lighter, better, newer, so she ran in and bought it, plus three more light jumpers and a matching scarf. Then she needed another coffee and cigarette and after that she popped into *Entertainment* and bought Freddy a laser gun.

She was quick – she was sure she was rushing – but by the time she got everything back to the car, it was almost twenty to five. Three missed calls. She rang Scott but it went to answerphone. She tried to take the roads carefully, but driving felt like flying.

At home, the front door was open. She dropped everything in the hall and refused to look at the man in the trilby who'd been standing there for weeks. Instead, she sped into the kitchen, tripping on a hammer. Scott cornered her by the sink.

"I think we should call Stemping."

She turned on the cold tap and took a cup from the draining board. It was dirty. There were stains in the corners, except they weren't corners because it was round. She couldn't think of the word. Cracks? Edges? Her sleeve was wet. She turned off the tap.

"Tessa? I said I think we should call Dr Stemping."

Calling Dr Stemping was the last thing she wanted to do.

Mothers all over West Sussex were making supper. There were glasses of wine being poured, there were pans on the boil and vegetables being chopped, there was last-minute homework on kitchen tables and sports kit being hurriedly washed, there was the thought for mothers everywhere that they were sick of cooking. But in Tessa's and Scott's house, no one was cooking anything.

She turned her attention to the freezer. It hurt her hands wrestling fish fingers from the frost. She shoved the peas back in, thought, *Peas,* and opened the freezer again. This time the bag split, sending *Sainsbury's basics* skittering across the floor like green pearls. They gathered in the crook of the hammer and found their way into the cupboard among splinters. How could she cook with the entire contents of the cupboard all over the table? Bowls, plates, cups; a city of cheap pottery waiting to fail. Where would Freddy eat? Even the fish fingers looked as if they'd given up. The packet was crushed, the cardboard wilted, a corner was dented in. Nothing ever turned out like it said it would; the promise of crispy breadcrumbs would be revealed as a disappointing lie. She threw them in the bin. She'd make pasta. She filled a pan with water. The rush of the tap was soothing, so she turned it on more, and then the hot tap, too. The pan overflowed; the sink began to fill. She went upstairs. What she needed was a bath.

She locked the bathroom door. Why was it such a mess? Why did the currents of her house throw up such refuse and ingrained smears of grease and soap? She turned the taps on full. Everything on the windowsill would have to go. Scott's coffee mug that he'd left there, toothpaste, face scrub, exfoliation glove, toothbrushes, *TePe* toothpicks – she swept the lot into the tub along with her make-up from the mirrored cabinet. Her *L'Oréal* cover-up, *Mac* foundation, powder brush, cotton wool pads, cleanser, toner, a rainbow of eye shadows, four mascaras, five lipsticks – all broken and bent – nail polish remover from *Boots* and six bottles of nail polish – three almost empty, all varying shades of pearl.

In they went among the rushing water where they bobbed and sank and seeped. What about Scott's shaving stuff? The badger brush and *classic men's foam* that she'd bought for him two Christmases ago, that he'd put back in the box and she'd taken out again and arranged on his shelf, that he'd used once and then gone back to his *Gillette*? She smashed the shelf in half and put the whole lot in the bin.

Her make-up turned the water green. It was so hot she had to take all her clothes off. She dropped them in the bath as well and put on her dressing gown. A car pulled up outside. She heard the crunch of wheels and slam of door.

She ran in her dressing gown, light as a sylph, from bathroom to hall to stairs and out into the garden without anyone seeing her. The cool of the grass felt wonderful under her feet – a refreshment from toes up. She ducked behind the yew hedge and found herself at the pond. *Ophelia,* she thought. Wading in, she lay quietly among reeds, her hands on her chest like a saint at rest, her head in the water as if her short blonde hair would drift in a wave of deep-red ripples around her. She could so easily go to sleep; she was so hot, the water so cool, she'd easily slip and go under. No one would find her. She could drift and sink, move with the pebbles beneath her back, the goldfish that brushed past her toes, she could turn to reed and stone and water, she could be found when this was over.

It was over the moment she opened her eyes and realised she was lying in the pond, her dressing gown open, a sharp cold piercing her veins. She jumped up and ran for the house. There were people, she could see them through the sitting room window, but she was too fast. Upstairs someone had turned off the taps. Where were her clothes? Her dressing gown sopping, weeds clinging, mud everywhere; she was freezing, shivering, her teeth a constant chatter. Where was Freddy? The question came to her suddenly. No one in her bedroom, she pulled on sweatpants and sweatshirt. They were all downstairs. Maybe they were having supper. She shook the last of the damp from her hair.

The kitchen looked like someone had taken a hammer to it. She went into the sitting room where she found Scott, standing at the window, smoking. His cigarette was almost out. She took it from him and took a drag.

"Is Freddy in bed?"

"Why don't you sit down?"

She wasn't sure if he was moving in the same reality as her; he drifted so quietly across the carpet, touching her arm, smiling. She didn't want to sit down.

"I need a cigarette."

"I'll roll you one."

He took his tobacco out of his pocket. She watched his hands moving slowly, expertly, such beautiful hands, hands she'd fallen in love with. When he put it between her lips and flicked his lighter, the flame jigged about so much that it was difficult to catch it. She burnt it halfway down the paper, the other half stayed unlit so that it stood up like a chimney in ruins. No drag, no satisfaction, her lungs tight, her breath shallow. She dropped it on the windowsill.

The doorbell went.

"I'll get it."

Scott touched her lightly at the base of her spine. "No. I'll get it."

She'd forgotten he was standing beside her. She'd thought she was in a cupboard; a close, dark space of not enough air, no way to breathe, bare brick against her back and a voice beyond the door. But she was in her sitting room and there were people coming in and standing in uncomfortable groups, edging at her with their eyes. Scott and Dr Stemping, two women in matching blue coats, a policewoman, and Clare. A bad drinks party with none of the people you want to see and all of the people you didn't, plus one friend who'd say after, *No, no, it was fine,* and clear up while you sat on the sofa and drank. Had she got them all together? She couldn't remember.

"Tess." Clare hugged her, or tried to, but the feel of someone near was too much, and Tessa moved instinctively to the side.

"Hi." She made it big and moved quickly to make it look like she was busy, which she was. No one had drinks. She hadn't changed. She was still in her sweatpants. But none of them looked dressed for a drinks party either, so maybe it was a 'come as you are'. Or were. That would be funny. She'd have to be three stone lighter and twenty-three years younger.

She needed her sunglasses. A dash for the coat stand, she crouched over her bag. The man in the trilby didn't move. Clare crouched beside her. "Let's take it into the sitting room." She picked it up. "What is it that you need?"

They sat beside each other on the sofa. Clare had the handbag on her lap. Tessa felt suddenly tired. If only these people would let her sleep for a minute, if only she could put on her sunglasses, but she couldn't find the energy to ask for them.

Scott sat on the coffee table in front of her, two pills in his hand. "Will you take your meds, Tessa?"

She jumped up and headed for the kitchen.

"Tess. We agreed. You agreed," he shouted after her.

The kitchen was no good. It was a mess. She didn't have her bag.

"Tessa." Dr Stemping moved towards her. "I want you to come and sit down."

Brown shoes, brown hair, that detestable stoop.

Everyone was looking at her; Clare on the sofa, Scott in the middle of the room, the two women in blue jackets, Dr Stemping one step closer, the policewoman – where was the policewoman? She was sure she'd been there. People were appearing and disappearing, and she couldn't make it out. The man in the trilby smiled. Tessa ran for the stairs. One of the women in blue jackets caught her as she reached the first step.

The rest was a blur for Tessa, a blur she knew too well. Arms held down, screaming, and crying and kicking at Scott and women in blue jackets. A strap too tight, an ambulance too bright, shouting and lights smacked with darkness, a sleep that gave no rest, a knowledge, deep inside, that she was dying. She struggled and kicked. She cried and pushed away, refused the drugs, and shouted at them to let her go. They never gave her enough time. They never let her be. They always interrupted as if they knew. They didn't understand she could see stars.

As the ambulance bumped away from her house and headed for the main road, Tessa, in the back, lolled quietly, the silence of trauma ringing changes with the rush of road beneath her.

2   I FEEL LOVE

24 hours earlier

It had started weeks ago; the tickle, the nudge, the grab, the feeling that she was hunted. A creeping sensation at her back, a sudden jerk awake in case it should catch her sleeping; she'd been feeling unwell for a while. A flutter through her veins, her heartbeat up a notch; through the darkness and boredom of everyday life it was the chink of a door just open, a light she could have, a promise of fun, the adrenalin rush of abandon. She could do what everyone else kept locked in a cupboard. She could break free. But it was ridiculous. Tessa, who had a home to a run, a child to love, a husband who needed his dinner. Tessa, who was a member of the home counties-based, middle-class community that drank too much, bragged about holidays, compared their children and flirted with each other's husbands. They didn't take hammers to cupboards, they didn't go mad; they got drunk and had sex, and behaved badly but laughed about it, badly like their parents before them. If they got fat, they cleansed, and if they were lonely or frightened or sad beyond repair, if the unhappiness in their heart and betrayal in their gut and madness in their soul rose up like a chemical explosion that threatened to ruin everything, they did up the kitchen. There was no time for the insistent nagging to kick down doors, break free. Nowhere was it written to smash walls. Tessa didn't have time for any of it. She had a house to tidy, a rugby match to get to, supper to think of.

A grey mist dampened the garden like an overcoat left out in the rain, great gulps of autumn had flattened the harvest and slowed to a miserable sniff. She'd had two hours' sleep but she'd figured it out completely. She'd move the cooker, put in an island, and redo the floor in slate. They'd have halogens and dinner parties and a sofa at the end. There'd be freshness and clean surfaces and, most of all, there'd be order. This sense of unrest, this feeling that something was wrong was down to crappy cupboards ruining her view. If she redid the kitchen, she'd feel better.

By half past eight, Freddy was running out the door, his school bag slung over his shoulder while Scott, a piece of toast in one hand, pushed him on, but Tessa, at the table, hadn't moved. She didn't expect him to talk to her, but a kiss would have been nice. She stared at the slick of milk that had washed up over Freddy's bowl of *Cheerios*. What she needed was a list.

She took her *Filofax* from the windowsill, slid the blue *Biro* from its leather loop, found an empty page and wrote *architect*. Then she crossed it out and wrote *builder*.

Get dressed or find a builder or tidy the breakfast away or get dressed. She walked in circles, picking up a fork, putting it down again. She rolled a cigarette and forgot to smoke it. She stared at the damp garden. By a quarter to twelve, all she'd managed was to remove one plate from the dishwasher. Her phone buzzed.

Me & Ros getting quick sandwich at pub. on way now. Come? x

*

In the tiny mirror of the cramped cubicle in the ladies' toilets of the White Horse, Tessa inspected her face, then her neck, then her waistline. She shouldn't have had the scampi. She should have had the salad, like Clare, or the club sandwich, like Ros. Then she wouldn't be feeling so fat. Outside her coffee was waiting for her. Hints of sunshine pushed through the clouds.

"Please can't one of you do it?" asked Clare. "I don't want it to be just me and Brian."

They'd been talking about *Blithe Spirit*, the latest production by the Midhurst Amateur Dramatics Society. Brian was the director.

"It won't just be you and Brian. Diane's in for Madam Arcati and I've said Issy can be the maid." Ros ripped a corner of Sweet'N Low with her teeth.

"You know what I mean. He's always suggesting we run lines together." Clare had sandy-brown hair cut like a scarecrow.

"He can't help it if he's in love with you," said Ros.

"He's lonely," said Tessa.

"He's a nutter," said Clare.

"He's kind," said Tessa. "I wish Scott was kind."

"You should do it, Tess," said Ros. "You'd be perfect for Elvira. You wouldn't have to rehearse."

"I'm not dead."

"But you are married."

"Only just." Tessa relit her roll-up.

"What happened?" asked Clare.

"I burnt the dinner."

"It's not 1953. I burn things all the time," said Ros.

"It was soup."

Ros and Clare laughed.

"Then you should definitely do the play. Show Scott what you're made of," said Ros.

"And you can teach me how to be his annoying other wife," said Clare.

"He only does the play to get away from me," said Tessa.

Ros picked up the teaspoon that Tessa had knocked to the grass when she'd tried to smoke a cigarette and drink her coffee at the same time. Blonde hair, shades of bombshell, fell over her face. She was so effortlessly pretty. She got a sparkly black clip out of her bag and twisted it up into a loose, messy chignon.

"What time tonight?" said Tessa.

"Seven-ish."

Ros got up. Clare and Tessa followed her. A BMW estate, a battered Subaru and Tessa's Range Rover were parked in a row. Ros opened her car door.

"And don't be late. Peter's determined to have a last barbecue effort, so I fucking hope it doesn't rain."

*

Home from the pub, Tessa made herself another coffee. It was hard to know her mind when it kept jumping about. She sat outside, the saturated sandbox at her feet. It had been the focus of last week's list, *Throw away/clean/donate to charity*. She hadn't done any of those things. Do the play. Don't do the play. Ask Scott if she should do the play. Tell Scott she was doing the play. Put the whole thing off until tomorrow. Ask Scott tonight. Don't mention it tonight. Ask him what he thought on their way to Peter and Diane's. Avoid talking about it completely. He blamed her; that was the problem. He said she didn't try hard enough.

She threw the dregs in the bushes. It had done her no favours. As she pulled on her boots by the coat stand, she pretended not to see the man in the trilby who'd been watching her. She put on a baseball cap and pulled it low over her eyes, picked up her bag and set off for Freddy's school.

The road from Midhurst to Billingshurst is one long shoot of the A272. It bends through Tillington, doglegs through Petworth and weaves round the corners of Wisborough Green, but if she imagined she was flying, then the effort was an arrow pointing east. She set off at speed leaving Midhurst behind as she flew the rise and fall of blind hills. Cowdray polo grounds fell away to her right, the golf course on her left gave way to woods. She looked in her rear-view mirror. There was a police car following her. It had tucked in behind her when she'd turned onto the main road and it hadn't swerved.

She rang Clare.

"Hi." She had to shout; she had the windows open.

"Hey." Clare's voice was distant. "Hang on a minute, Tess."

There was a clatter of buckets or maybe it was the wind, or maybe she imagined it.

"Clare?"

"Give me a minute, hang on."

"There's a police car following me."

"Hang on, Tess. A what?"

"A police car. It's been on my tail the whole way."

"Hang on." A door banged and Clare's voice became clearer. "Where are you?"

"On my way to school."

"Should it be following you?"

"I don't know."

"I mean, is it following you? Are you sure it's not just behind you?"

"It's been on me the whole way."

"But it's not doing anything?"

"It won't get off my tail."

"Are you hands-free? And you haven't jumped a light or something? Are you speeding?"

"They're wearing hats."

"Hats?"

"Their hats."

"Does it matter?"

"They only wear hats when it's serious." She veered around a motorbike and kept her speed exactly at the limit. "It doesn't matter." It was difficult to concentrate. She cut the call and checked her rear-view mirror again. The police switched on their lights; the blue siren flash filled her brain. She slowed, they indicated, sped up and overtook her.

She steadied her breathing. Calm. Be calm. She kept her eyes on the road as it dipped and rose beneath her. As she crested the next hill, she saw a zebra run into the forest and be lost among trees.

She held on tight to the steering wheel. She tried very hard to breathe, but her hands were sweating and her chest was tight. She turned on the radio. 'I Feel Love' swept into the car.

3 SOMEBODY SMASHED UP THE KITCHEN

"What time are we supposed to be there?" Scott shouted up the stairs.

She'd got home at six with Freddy covered in mud, a trophy in his hands, her arms full of homework and sports bag and water bottle. She'd kicked the car door shut with such force she'd left a dent in it.

"I'm coming."

He knew perfectly well what time. It was his way of pointing out they were late. She picked up a flowery smock and held it against her. Too flimsy. She tried on a wrap dress for the third time, took it off and threw it on the floor.

"Barbara's here. We have to go."

Into the uncomfortable Land Rover, she brushed pine needles from the seat, gripped the dashboard with one hand and slammed the door with the other. Her crappy white jeans were already covered in sawdust, her tunic made her arms look like hams, and her cardigan was crumpled on her lap.

"Don't slam it."

He always had to remind her. She always forgot. He put the engine into gear. She didn't bother wrestling with the seat belt; it was a strap with no give, designed in South Africa when they were considered unnecessary. He never did his up either. He used to run overland from Cape Town to Cairo, the back full of travellers, the roof loaded with tents, but had retrained as a tree surgeon and moved to West Sussex. Her first view of him had been of his legs dangling from a branch in her mother's garden. He'd told her the bone rattle had got to him. She used to think it was romantic.

"Did you remember the bottle?"

Freddy hadn't needed one in years. "He'll eat your lasagne."

"Of wine."

She looked pointlessly in the back, at the harness and chainsaw, the petrol cans, his steel-capped boots, then between her feet and in her bag. At the junction he veered into the BP garage, screeched to a halt, got out and slammed the door. It was all right for him to do it, apparently. She watched him cross the forecourt and stride into the brightly lit interior. He glanced in her direction once, not at her, but casually as if idling the time.

A bottle of Jacob's Creek on her lap, they set off again.

She held the neck. "I'm thinking of doing the play."

He veered right onto the road to Tillington.

"Scott?"

"I heard you."

"What do you think?"

"Do what you want."

"But do you want me to do it?" She felt like she was talking to an angry, petulant child with good hair and an accent that drove women crazy. She used to make him say 'owl' and 'mirror' for a laugh. He said he'd picked Midhurst out with a pin, anything but the crowded world of Northern Ireland. She suspected he liked being different.

"You'll have to audition."

"Don't be a shit."

"I'm just saying."

"You're just saying there are two parts left and you don't want me to do either of them."

"Which one are you thinking of doing?"

"Your wife, obviously. I'm not going to be Brian's wife."

"I'd rather not play your husband on stage as well as off."

"You are my husband. I thought it might be good for us."

The way he laughed made Tessa hate him.

*

Ros's brother owned the Rectory, converted from pokey to large. The drive was crowded with Range Rovers, Hondas, Audis and Mitsubishis, and Peter's Porsche was hemmed into a corner of gravel. The noise of the party spilled out through the open front door.

"Scotty!" Ros, a martini in one hand, a *Marlboro* in the other, put her arms around Scott's neck. "Darling." She waved the cigarette hand at Tessa.

They followed her perfectly tight arse through the Rectory kitchen where vicars' wives had felt shut in, but which now stretched from front to back with large glass doors to a garden that had grown like the house to double that after Peter bought the fields next door. On the terrace, the complete collection of Midhurst society stood about in groups. Tessa wasn't sure if she should turn over the drinks table or take the glass of Chablis Peter offered her and ask him how his summer was.

"Oh, Christ, you know." Peter kissed her on both cheeks. "Usual bloody bore. Scotto! Jim Beam." He handed Scott a glass and they headed off to the rugby dads, who were standing around the cooling barbecue, the last few chicken drumsticks, one lonely burger on a plate.

Tessa found Clare among the mums, the women with whom she'd been through childbirth and nursery, birthday parties and cystitis. "Hey."

"Hey. You look great." Clare kissed her.

Tessa took the lighter from Clare. Her skin felt too thin, her head too high. They were talking about Diane's kitchen.

"So practical."

"But will it work with a ground-source heat pump?"

"Apparently you have to change the pipes."

Their faces had a sheen like wax. Their mouths were disturbing. Tessa saw Diane bearing down on another group who'd been in Midhurst long enough to have given up comparing houses. Perhaps, thought Tessa, she, too, would be happier when she was old. She left Clare's side and met Diane on the lawn.

"Tessy." She kissed Tessa's cheek. A tray of cupcakes in one hand, a bottle in the other, she offered both. "Top-up or food?"

Over on the bench by the willow tree, Scott had got talking to Brian.

"Here she is," said Brian.

Tessa's mouth was full. She held up her glass in greeting.

"Come and sit." He patted three inches of bench.

He always appeared to Tessa as if there were two of him, one squashed inside the other. The outer wore tweed and had a firm gut, the inner had something of the killer to it. He'd fought in the second Iraq war and whenever she looked at him, all she could think was Abu Ghraib. He'd been a farmer for the last fifteen years. He supplied Cowdray Farm Shop with beef.

"How's the play?"

"Scott tells me I've stolen his babysitter. Thought he was talking about you!"

"Barbara's agreed to be Mrs Bradman," said Scott.

"Still searching for my Elvira, though. You'd think they'd be queuing up."

"I was thinking of auditioning."

"Tessa!" Brian spilled his beer. "I didn't know it was your thing. We'd love to have you."

"It's not her thing," said Scott.

"Now, now." Brian patted Scott's knee.

"What's going on?" asked Clare, joining them.

"Tessa's going to be in the play."

"I didn't say I was going to be in it."

"Oh, thank God." Clare raised her glass.

"I said I'd audition."

"You won't need to audition," said Brian.

"That's what I said," said Clare. She reclaimed her lighter from Tessa's back pocket.

"It should be Ros doing it," said Tessa.

"She won't do it," said Clare.

"Have you asked her?" said Scott.

"She's a professional," said Tessa.

"It's only am-dram," said Scott.

"Now, look here," said Brian, "let's be straight. It may only be am-dram, but we do like to take it seriously."

Clare closed her eyes and Scott laughed.

"Oi, oi, everyone." Ros came wheeling over and shoved herself between Scott and Brian, making them shuffle up.

Scott turned at an angle and stretched his arm along the back of the bench.

"Scott wants you to be his wife," said Tessa.

"I say," said Ros, squirming against him.

"Elvira," added Tessa.

"Oh, don't be stupid. Me and Clare just spent the whole of bloody lunch trying to persuade Tess to do it. Christ, you two are big. I can't breathe. Somebody help me up." She stuck her arms and legs out like a child. Clare looked for somewhere to put her drink.

"They trying to get you in the play?" said Peter, arriving among them and pulling Ros to her feet. "You know she'll take over."

"Of course I won't," said Ros. "Anyway, they don't need me."

"Yes, we do," said Scott.

"She'll act you off the stage," said Peter, handing Brian another beer.

"Exactly," said Scott. "It'd be stupid to have Tess do it. We're already married. We need a bit of fizz."

"Are there a lot of lines?" asked Tessa.

"It's the lead," said Scott, rubbing his face.

"You'll be fine," said Brian.

"All you need is chemistry," said Ros.

"Exactly," said Scott.

*

Tessa didn't remember going to bed, but she remembered waking at two-seventeen, three forty-six and almost five when she crept away from a sleeping Scott and lay in the bath watching the slow seep of water drench the wall from a leak in the roof. When it was light and Freddy stirred, asked for *Cheerios* and settled in front of his *PlayStation,* she made Scott a cup of coffee.

"I was thinking about the kitchen." She sat on the bed.

"Not now, Tess."

"I was thinking about moving the cooker."

"We already made a decision."

"But did you see Diane's cupboards?"

"Their kitchen's twice the size." He took the cup from her. His hair stuck out at angles and his eyes were sleepy.

"I could put in an island."

"We won't have any space."

"And underfloor heating."

He pushed off the covers. A waft of warmth and stale sweat came with him.

"Why don't you want me to do the play?"

"Fred." He knocked on Freddy's door.

"He's downstairs." Tessa followed him to the bathroom, his broad back, the scar where a tent pole had glanced through his skin, hit his shoulder blade, left a rivulet of tissue that she'd traced with her finger on the night they'd first had sex. So long ago; a tenderness lost. When had he stopped touching her? He left his cup on the bathroom windowsill and lifted the lid on the loo. His piss stank of beer and salt.

"Do you think Ros is better looking than me?"

"For fuck's sake, Tess."

"Is that why you want her to do the play?"

"I want her to do it because she's good." He turned on the shower.

"And I'm not?" She flushed the loo.

"She's a professional."

"It's only am-dram."

"Then you fucking do it. I'm not standing in your way. Brian said you've got the part; Ros doesn't want it. Maybe I won't do it. Maybe I'll tell Brian to cast someone else as Charles."

But he was standing in her way. He was blocking the light and preventing her from breathing. He stepped out of his pants and left them, crotch up, on the floor.

"I won't do it if you're not doing it."

"Fine."

"Don't go thinking she fancies you."

"I don't."

"But you think I'm not good enough."

"I never said that." He pushed past her to the airing cupboard.

"You said there were a lot of lines."

"Are there no fucking towels?"

She handed him Freddy's Donald Duck swimming towel. "She'd do it if you persuaded her."

"Please, Ros, not now."

"You called me Ros."

"I meant Tessa. Tessa, Jesus."

"You said Ros." She took a step forward as he slid open the shower, but he shut it in her face.

*

He took Freddy to rugby practice. The house was quiet. Pick up wet towels and pull out clean washing and get out the ironing board and change her mind and leave everything stranded in the hall. Every time she was about to ring the builder, she remembered it was Sunday. Every time she

21

looked at the washing, it was too much, so she got a hammer from the toolbox instead.

The dividing wall to the playroom was thinner than she'd expected – the hammer went straight through. The sitting room could be a problem. She tried hitting a space under the cupboard that stored plates and mugs. She turned the hammer sideways to get a good shot, but it bounced, almost hitting her in the face, and where she'd struck there was hardly a dent. Maybe if she took the cupboard off the wall, she could get a proper shot. She unscrewed the door. The mugs and plates, she put on the table. She should have done this years ago; the shelves were a fucking mess, dusty and stained. If she took the whole thing off and took it outside, she could spray it with the hose.

It was heavier than expected and as the last screw loosened, it tipped sideways and fell forwards, almost knocking her over. She had to let go otherwise her back would have broken. It crashed onto the counter, sending *Cheerios* scattering, and fell to the floor almost hitting her toes. Her shin was grazed; she saw a trickle of blood, but there wasn't much pain, hardly any, just a graze and a trickle, and a splintered cupboard on the floor showing layers of dust on its top – a dust that no one got to. Tessa put the screwdriver down and went up to the bathroom. The shower cubicle needed cleaning. The cheap concertina doors that Scott had slammed had mould growing up the inside. She kicked a panel and broke it.

There are eddies in a house, on a windowsill, a dressing table, just outside a door where things collect. Tessa found herself moving with this current, from bathroom to bedroom to landing, being curled among hair clips and coins, a sock in a doorway, a plastic sword left poking through bannisters.

She could almost close her eyes and be carried with it, its force was so strong. It lifted her from hall to waterfall of stairs. It moved her gracefully as if swirled and danced, no longer in charge, had she ever been. Music played incessantly; songs of childhood that spoke of how things ought to be. She was beautiful. She was cared for. When she opened her eyes, she'd landed by the fridge. Somebody had smashed up the kitchen, so Tessa went shopping.

4   YOU'LL TAKE THE PART

In her sweet little cottage on the edge of Petworth Park, Ros was happy. How could she not be? She had her dogs, her girls, a home, a social life. Molly and Issy had settled into their new school; Molly had made friends and Issy didn't seem to need any. Maybe she'd grow out of her father's features; maybe, with distance, her youngest daughter would stop with the looks that made Ros feel guilty about everything.

Harold had been a mistake. If she could change anything, she'd have her girls with a different father, one who wouldn't cause her such pain. She'd still be divorced, but divorced from someone pliant, or dead – that would be better. It was her who'd been too pliant, doing anything to keep the peace. She was the one who'd had to grow up, grow a pair, stand up for herself for a change. If he'd stop being such a cunt for just one minute, she wouldn't have to keep fighting so hard.

But it was only now and then; a smoulder in the background that occasionally caught fire. At forty-six, a new house, a new life, a new set of friends she could be her new self; go where she wanted, see who she wanted, be free of judgement. She still saw her analyst in West London, but she'd come to enjoy her old haunts. Sometimes she had lunch in Daylesford Café. Last time, she'd bumped into her dealer. He'd followed her to *Wild at Heart* and made a joke about the killing dullness of the countryside while she chose between peonies and azaleas, so she'd sat in his car and bought a gram of coke. The countryside wasn't lonely. It was fun, especially if you were single.

She pulled on her boots, took the leads from the hook, Crosby and Nash bounced beside her. Through the gate in the wall and Petworth Park rolled out in green and misty damp, the rise of parkland trees caught like ghosts lingering in the growing light. What a glorious place to live, how lucky she was, she hardly missed London at all. Her cottage was a bit tumbledown, but Peter had said he'd do it up in time, and she was welcome to get out a paintbrush. He'd have bought it anyway; places like that didn't come up very often and at the time she'd have lived anywhere. She'd had to get out. Everything had fallen down around her.

At drama school, they'd said she was going to be a star. She would have been if she hadn't met Harold. He was at law school; she was playing Miss Prism at *The Gate*. In his funny glasses and bright-blue suit, she'd thought he looked like Austin Powers. *I'm on my way to the bar,* he'd shouted in the uproar of the after-party. *I'll have a gin and tonic,* she'd shouted back. It had been the first and last joke between them.

They'd bought a house in West London. Her brother had helped with her side. She'd meant to get back to her career after Molly but then she got pregnant with Issy. Once in a while she met with her drama school friends in bistros in Covent Garden, where they reminded her how brilliant she was, while she replied that she really loved being a mother. She couldn't talk to her friends about Harold, they all thought she had The Life. She'd tried talking to Peter, she'd even tried talking to her own mother, but they'd both said she was lucky to have him. With both girls settled at primary school, she'd finally got the parts that meant something to her; a year on *Casualty* and a run at the Old Vic playing Masha in *Three Sisters* turned out to be her peak. Award shows in Leicester Square, excitable mothers at pick-up, she'd had it for a while and then she'd given it all away. She told herself she was over it. Autographs in the playground could only go so far. The thought made her happy half the time.

The grass sprang, the dogs bounced and the sun shone, lifting the white glaze of morning. She walked home, thoughts of putting her feet up on her mind. She hadn't heard from Tessa or Clare for a couple of days. Usually, one or the other called her. They were all right, the Midhurst lot. Nothing special but nothing awful either. Clare was sweet. Ros couldn't get over how little she cared about her appearance, but if you ran the stables and didn't have any money, she supposed there wasn't time. Still, a little blusher, and a brush of that scarecrow hair, heels once in a while, something other than shapeless tops – surely that wasn't too much of a stretch. She couldn't want to be alone forever. And Tessa was a bit… she avoided using the word *fat* even in the privacy of her own mind. She wasn't that person. Instead, she daydreamed about getting her on a fitness regime that involved aloe vera.

*

At six o'clock that evening, after a day of not doing much, her phone buzzed.

At pub. Come? x

Molly and Issy, home from school, were both shut in their rooms apparently doing homework. Ros shouted up the stairs that she'd only be an hour and drove to the White Horse, where she found Clare in the beer garden with Scott.

"You two look happy." They were hunched and smoking, their expressions tight. "What's happened? Someone called off the play?"

"Tessa's in hospital," said Scott.

Ros sat down. "What's happened?" She meant it this time.

"She's had an episode," said Clare.

"She's been sectioned," said Scott.

"For what?" Ros lit a *Marlboro*.

"For being fucking mental."

"That's not fair," said Clare.

"It's not really fair that she smashed up the kitchen either." Scott scratched the back of his neck.

"You're going to have to catch me up here," said Ros. "What do you mean, she's been sectioned?"

"It means," said Scott, "she's gone properly off her fucking nut, trashed the house and thrown herself in the pond. She'll blame me. You know she's going to blame me."

"There was nothing you could do," said Clare.

"I know that, but it won't make any fucking difference, will it? It was me that called the police."

"The police?" said Ros.

"You had no choice," said Clare.

"Unless she takes her pills and checks herself in voluntarily, which she never does, they arrest her, section her and she gets a bed. I got Stomper over."

"Who's Stomper?" asked Ros.

27

"Dr Stemping. Her psychiatrist. You have to. I did it by the book. I always do it by the fucking book and I always get blamed for it."

"I'll back you up, you know, when she comes out." Clare sipped her drink.

"Stemping always freaks her out, anyway. It never works. I don't know why I bother."

"Jesus," said Ros. "But what made her freak out? I mean, what happened? A person doesn't just go off their nut—"

"She's bipolar," said Clare.

"Hides it well, doesn't she?" said Scott.

"She doesn't hide it that well," said Clare.

"She does if you don't know her."

"I'd no idea," said Ros.

"She doesn't like anyone to talk about it," said Scott.

"She's protecting Freddy," said Clare.

"I should have brought him round to yours. I had his bag packed." Scott rubbed his eyes.

"You could have called me," said Ros.

"That's sweet of you, but me and Clare have been through this before. This is what…" He looked at Clare. He had sawdust in his hair and lines around his mouth. "Fourth since Freddy?"

Clare counted on her fingers. "I think this is her seventh since you got together." She opened her tobacco, tore a square from the flip top of the *Rizlas* and rolled it into a filter. "She doesn't like taking the medication."

Ros passed her the lighter. "Doesn't she have to?"

"She doesn't have to do anything until they section her," said Scott. He drained the last of his beer.

"She doesn't like the weight gain," said Clare.

"It's not the pills that make her put on weight, it's the not doing any fucking exercise and not doing a fucking thing to help herself and sitting around eating cake."

"She doesn't sit around eating cake." Clare put the lighter back on the table between them. A corner of the sticker on its side was wrinkled. Ros picked at it with her fingernail.

"She doesn't do fuck all else," said Scott.

"You're just angry. You know it's not her fault."

"I do not know that." Scott pushed his empty glass away from him. "I know she's got an illness, but there's more to it than falling over when it hits her. There's the telling us, there's the telling Stomper, there's waving that white flag we all agreed on. There's the taking her fucking medication. But does she do it? Does she fuck. And whose fault is that?"

"Do you think she's been throwing them away?"

"Why would she do that?" asked Ros. "I mean, surely she can find some that don't make her put on weight. If she's got an illness, then doesn't she—"

"She doesn't like the label."

"On the box?" said Ros.

Scott laughed. "You're funny."

"Of being bipolar," said Clare.

"Oh, oh sorry, of course. Sorry." Ros ripped off the sticker and crushed it between her fingers. "It was just that I thought that everyone was talking about mental health these days. You know that it was out in the open? She needs to know that she's not alone." She dropped the crumpled sticker on the grass.

"Yeah, well, that's all well and good for Twitter and Facebook and Radio fucking Four, but for those of us actually living with it, it's not something you want batted around the supermarket, or at least it isn't for Tessa. This isn't some cute little panic attack at the deli counter, this is psychosis. Her problem isn't that she's bipolar, it's that she thinks she's not." Scott stood up. "Another?" He pointed at Clare's glass.

"Me too, please." Ros swirled the ice in the last of her gin and tonic.

"Let me tell you." Scott straddled the bench, one leg in, one leg out. "She's going to have to deal with that fucking label now. This is the last time, Clare. I swear to it. I'm not going through this again." He marched off across the grass.

Clare raised her eyebrows and pressed her lips together.

"Wow," said Ros.

"He'll be okay. He's just frustrated, you know? It's hard loving someone with…" Clare shook her head. "They've been through it so many times, and now with Freddy…"

It was a beautiful evening, as the morning had been, warm as if summer was making a last stab at being remembered. The pub garden filled up; smoke drifted into the air. Plates of *White Horse* burgers and fish and chips were eaten at wonky tables, cutlery and condiments picked up from the green dresser by the door.

"Have you eaten?" Clare rubbed her hands back and forth through her hair and combed it down with her fingers.

"I'll eat later with the girls." She'd left a shepherd's pie defrosting on the *Aga*. "What white flag is he talking about?"

"We agreed last time that if any of us thought she was getting ill, or if she felt it was coming, that she'd let us know so we could head it off at the pass. Up her meds, take the pressure off, whatever was pressing in on her. She could go out to her mum and dads for a bit."

"Did you know she was ill?" Ros touched the lighter where the sticker had been, a trace of a label that would gather dust and become annoying.

"I had a feeling. She rang me after that lunch we had here. She was on her way to Freddy's match. She said there was a police car following her. Always with the police or the CIA, or she's pregnant, or there's a flood – they're the signs. Sometimes I think she likes it. She'll have known for ages."

Scott returned with a pint of bitter, a half of Guinness, a gin and tonic and three packets of crisps. He opened one and spilled it onto the table. "Will you do it then?" He looked at Ros with those deep-green eyes of his.

"Do what?"

"The play. Did you not ask her, Clare? Clare was worried about the play."

"I was not."

"Clare wants you to do it."

"I didn't say that."

"In Tessa's place?"

"Of course in fucking Tessa's place."

"Scott," said Clare.

"Sorry. Just tired. Yes. In Tessa's place. It'd solve that problem, anyway."

"We could say you're standing in," said Clare, "and then carry on, and—"

"Hope no one notices?" said Scott.

"If we say she's not doing it, they'll want to know why. They'll want to go and see her, in hospital. I mean, if we say she's in hospital. We could say she's suffering from exhaustion and gone to stay with her parents."

"Or her parents are suffering from exhaustion and she's gone to make it worse."

"You're a funny man, Scott," said Clare, not laughing. She picked up her Guinness.

"It doesn't matter. We'll think of something. Will you do it, Ros?"

"It'd be a big help," said Clare.

"Well, I guess… I mean, Issy's in it."

"There you go then," said Scott.

"But she might not—"

"She'd love to have her mam along, wouldn't she? Show us all how it's done?"

"I was going to say that Tessa might not like it."

"Tessa doesn't know shit right now and the last thing she's going to care about is the play."

She wasn't making herself understood. She'd been here before, that was the thing; they always said no one minded, but they did. It was never *just a play*.

"It's just a play, Ros," said Clare. "It really would help."

"You'll be grand," said Scott.

"Okay, okay!" She held up her hands in mock surrender. "I'll do it. Anyway," she touched Clare's wrist lightly, "that's the least of our worries. Poor you two. What a nightmare. I wish you'd called me."

"There wouldn't have been anything you could have done." Clare moved her arm away and scratched where Ros had touched it.

"And we're used to it," added Scott.

But they'd had all week.

They finished their drinks. Scott and Clare got up to leave, Ros followed, kissing them both goodbye in the car park. Before she set off, the engine running, she dialled Brian's number but changed her mind and cut the call before it started to ring.

5   LYING TO PETER AND DIANE

Ros and her girls were round for Sunday lunch at her brother's. She'd shut Crosby and Nash in the boot room to stop them ransacking the beef. Her brother had said, *Getting the full West Sussex kit, are we?* when she'd turned up last year with two black Labrador puppies in a cage. *They're for Molly and Issy,* she'd snapped back. Christmas presents that had turned into more work for her. They'd been so sweet aged eight weeks. *You'll have to take them gun dog training,* Peter had replied, turning to the culture section of the *Financial Times*. She'd told him to fuck off. He could talk with his glass walkway and 4WD Porsche. As if he had the rights to all of it.

"Have more potatoes." She'd been watching Molly stall at the loaded platters that crowded the centre of the large dining room table. Cabbage richly mixed with chestnuts and lardons; roast beef, pink and thinly sliced; Yorkshire puds like golden clouds exploding. A pile of roast potatoes, honeyed parsnips, glazed carrots, Peter's home-made horseradish in a bowl, but Molly's plate looked like an art piece from the eighties when a parsley leaf did for supper. "Give yourself some gravy."

"She's fine, Mum."

At least Issy ate. Even if she refused to say anything nice, at least some goodness went in her mouth.

"Get your fingers out of the horseradish." Ros leaned across her youngest daughter to get at the cabbage. She held up a spoon, but Molly moved her plate away. She could hear the dogs scratching at the boot room door. "Can we give them a bone, or something?"

Her brother went off to the kitchen. He still had his Nick Cave apron on. Sunday lunch was his domain and he didn't mind who knew it. A bit like the countryside in general. He'd said, *It's a quiet life here, Ros. I'm not sure you'll like it,* but he didn't know shit. She hadn't had this much attention in years. Her analyst had asked her if she wanted to get married again and she'd said if he could see her social life, he wouldn't bother. She watched the marrieds, the wives bitter, the husbands fat, and think *Thank God, what hell, no thanks.* Her brother and his wife seemed the only ones happy.

"Pass your plate." She held the spoon towards Molly.

"Leave her alone." Diane topped up Ros's glass. "Girls that age never eat."

"Mum never eats." Issy dipped her finger in the horseradish again.

"She did at your age," said Peter, coming back in. "Quite the porker."

Ros threw him a look. "Molly. Give me your plate."

"I can do it myself." Molly took the spoon out of her mother's hand. Long brown hair, a fringe Ros used to push away when she was still allowed to touch her.

"And the bacon and chestnuts. Not just the cabbage."

"I'm seventeen, Mum. I can do it."

"Do leave her." Diane put a reassuring hand on Molly's arm. "You're fine, darling."

"Were you fat, Mum?" asked Issy.

"How's school, Molly?" asked Peter.

"She's predicted three A stars," said Ros. Having a rich brother had its pluses and minuses. On the one hand, he'd bought her a house and paid for the girls' schooling. On the other, he'd bought her a house and paid for the girls' schooling. A gift with one, an expectation with the other, they all had to be happy, the girls had to succeed, he'd never been cornered like she had. Ros watched her brother's face and hoped for approval. His life had rolled out in steps he was willing to take; Westminster, Cambridge, Goldman Sachs and when their father had died, Peter had inherited everything. Her mother had said countless times, *You were only fifteen, Roselyn. Daddy did what he thought was best.* Daddy could have realised she'd grow up and not want to be dependent on her brother for the rest of her life. *There's nothing to stop you getting a job.* She'd heard that one, too. She'd had a job; she'd had a brilliant job doing what she loved best. It wasn't her fault it had ended.

"None of it makes a sou of difference," said Diane. "You pass, you fail, it's only school. Careers told me there was no business in jumpers!" Diane had run a knitting company and sold it for millions.

"It does make some difference," said Peter.

"It's where you go that matters."

"Where did you go?" said Issy.

"Cheltenham Ladies." Diane took another slice of beef. "And then Cambridge." She smiled at Molly.

Bloody Diane. If she hadn't mentioned it, Molly might have been content with something lower. Like Southampton. Or Exeter.

"She's quite right, of course." Peter passed Molly

the gravy. "Get a third at Cambridge, you still went to Cambridge."

"You've still got to get into Cambridge," said Molly.

"You'll get in," said Diane.

"I might not."

"You're a bright girl," said Peter.

"I want to go to Bedales," said Issy. She was blonde like Harold had been when he was a little boy. Bloody endless trips to his mother's house, the adored son, photographs of him everywhere.

"You don't want to stay at Seaford, Iss?"

Issy shook her head. "Bedales, then RADA or Bristol Old Vic."

Ros flapped her napkin. "Issy's got a thing about acting."

"Good for you," said Diane.

"Anyone can act," said Issy. "I want to direct."

"Not everyone can act." Ros sliced a carrot in half. "I've told her it's a tough business."

"Issy's tough," said Peter.

"Do you not like your friends?" said Diane.

"I did say it was the wrong place for her." Peter tore his Yorkshire pudding in half.

"Will you come and look with me?" Issy scooped up a bit of cabbage that was hanging from her mouth.

"I can do that," said Ros.

"I'd like Uncle Peter to do it. He's paying the bills."

There were pluses and minuses to being upfront with your kids, too.

"Dad said he'll pay uni fees, if I get in," said Molly.

"When did you speak to your dad?" asked Ros.

Molly moved a lardon from one side of her plate to the other. "Nancy says she'll have to get a loan."

"Has she not got a rich dad?" said Issy.

Ros glared at her. All she'd gathered from Clare was that Nancy's dad wasn't around. She'd had to guess the rest.

"Will Dad pay for Bedales, too?"

"I'm not taking money from him, full stop," said Ros.

"Isn't it up to Peter?" said Diane.

"It's up to me and Peter. If you want to change schools, that's fine, but we need to discuss it."

"We are discussing it," said Issy.

"Some other time," said Ros.

"Why not now?" insisted Issy.

"Because Peter wants his lunch."

"I'm sure he's capable of eating and talking at the same time, aren't you, darling?" said Diane. She filled the chair, the table, the room with her mass of scarves and beads and open arms. A constant forgiveness. Ros would do anything to see her snap.

"I want to have my lunch then. Molly, have some carrots."

"I don't want carrots."

"Did I tell you, Diane," Ros picked up her glass of wine, "that Brian's asked me to do the play?"

"I thought you turned it down."

"I changed my mind."

"You're going to be in the play?" asked Issy.

"As Elvira."

"But I'm in the play."

"I thought Tessa was Elvira," said Diane.

"She's asked me to step in."

"You just said Brian asked you to step in."

"I've had quite enough of you for one day, Miss Busy."

Issy made a face and Peter laughed.

"She's asked me to hold the fort."

"I don't want to do the play with you."

"Won't it be fun to do something together?" said Diane.

"No," said Issy.

"Don't lick your knife." Ros emptied her glass and reached for the bottle.

"Next time I'm going to give you just horseradish," said Peter.

"I'd like that," said Issy, licking her knife again.

"There's no reason why we shouldn't have two Elviras," said Diane.

"How can there be two Elviras?" said Issy.

"Finish your lunch," said Ros.

"And we'd be thrilled to have you. You'll be a boon," added Diane, slopping gravy down her front.

"No she won't."

Diane wiped her shirt. With so much pattern, it was hard to see what was what. "Your mother's a professional, Isabel. We're jolly lucky to have her. You should have seen us last year."

"I did see you last year." Ros put her knife and fork together.

"It was very sweaty," said Issy.

"Can I get down?" said Molly. Her fringe was almost in her eyes. She pushed her hair over her shoulder.

"You've hardly eaten anything."

"You're fine, Moll," said Diane. "You too, Isabel."

"Don't you want pudding?" Ros picked Issy's napkin off the floor.

"Have a brownie," said Diane. "They're in the larder."

"But don't let the dogs out," Ros called after Issy's departing back.

"Can I take it home? I have homework," said Molly, reappearing with a brownie in her hand.

After the door slammed, Ros put her feet up on Issy's chair and finished off the red.

"I'll let them out into the garden," said Peter, getting up.

"Everything all right then?" Diane began stacking plates.

"You can see what I have to put up with. She's like a bird."

"I meant with Tessa."

Outside the window, Crosby and Nash raced into view and tumbled over each other on the lawn. Peter still accused her of not walking them enough. He had all the time in the world. She couldn't see why he didn't do it. The table was a mess of plates and half-empty dishes, most of the beef, all of the horseradish, only a scattering of cabbage left. The platters, painted with pheasants, were part of a set from their childhood that Peter had also inherited, as if their mother never thought Ros would have a table big enough. She stretched her arms over her head, her spine against the chair. God, she was tired. She grappled for her cigarettes.

"Would you mind?" Diane set sail for the doorway, a platter in each hand.

Ros got up, a *Marlboro* already between her lips. In the garden, she leaned in through the kitchen window as Peter and Diane made coffee and loaded the dishwasher. "She's had to sort something parental." Smoke clouded and vanished above her.

"Nothing serious, I hope?" Diane took a bowl out and rearranged the plates.

"God, no. You know Tess, she's terribly close to her mother."

"Is she?"

Ros had no idea. Most people were. "Her father's broken his toe or something. She'll be back soon."

"I should hope so." Diane snapped the dishwasher shut and turned it on.

Ros lost what she said next. She'd gone over to the *Aga* where Peter was warming milk, but she heard Peter say, 'How should I know?'

She stubbed her cigarette out on the windowsill where it left a smear. "Can I help?"

Diane had started on the roasting pan. The tap was running, the sink filled with suds, Diane had her sleeves up. A year, and they still treated her like an errant schoolgirl sent home on suspension, as if she was expected to be taking a long, hard look at herself for something she hadn't done. What did they know about life? They'd met, married, decided against children; they'd had it easy from day one. Ros leaned in at the window again. "You must let me bring something next time, Di. I could do my beef stew, give you a Sunday off."

"Coffee," said Peter, lifting a tray from the island.

"I'll come in," said Ros.

"Do mind the agapanthus," said Diane, shutting the window.

MERCURY WARD

Tessa rang Scott from the payphone. Strange they still had one. A real old payphone with a clunky slit for a ten pence piece and that beep-beep sound. Weird.

"It was the man in the trilby." She had to get it out quickly in case they stopped her. She'd known that happen; the line go mysteriously dead, or whir, a purr as if someone else was listening. "Can you hear me?" she whispered, but Scott breathed that long, slow out-breath that drove her crazy. It didn't matter. She had to get the information across. "I think he was CIA."

"Okay, okay." At last, his voice, steady, samey, she couldn't tell if he'd taken it in.

"Okay." She replaced the receiver. Leaned against the wall.

Her slippers were pink, old and soft. Shuffle, shuffle to her room, her shins pale and hairy, a shallow gash that had dried to a rivulet of blood; a middle-aged mess sticking out of black leggings that stopped below the knee, her feet disappeared into the faded mules. Scott had brought them in instead of her white ones. Not the feet, the slippers.

Her room was trashed. It was amazing she hadn't broken

the window. Desk down on its knees, bed pulled away from the wall, mattress in a backflip.

"We wanted you to see it before we cleaned it up." Nurse Ratchet stood behind her. They all looked the same after a while if you'd been in enough. Half of them knew her by name. *All right, Tessa. Back again, are we?* they'd said when she'd arrived.

She sat on the floor among the chaos, on the small piece of floor that was left. She sat with her legs crossed as if she were a schoolgirl, as if it were morning assembly. When had it started? When had she got so ill that she'd never got better, been so covered in the slime of mental illness that every slice of her dripped with it? The first time it happened, they'd said it was the pot that had flipped her head. *Like the mattress*, she thought, staring at it. Too much pot and not enough sleep, an excitable constitution and a weak and faulty brain that misfired chemicals and made her crazy. Nothing to do with her sisters shutting her in a cupboard when she was six. Nothing to do with them giving her magic mushrooms and whispering through the door that she was dead. There was much from her childhood that she couldn't remember, but she'd never forgotten that hour – or was it five minutes or was it forever? The scratch of brick on her bare shoulder, the empty light-bulb socket that knocked her head, the memory of dust and swirl of air claustrophobic, the taste of earth from the mushroom they'd made her eat. *Go on, Tess, don't be a baby, you can be like Alice in Wonderland.* A repeating pattern of feelings that had not let her be, a connecting tissue she'd tried to break. But it was hardly the basis for a lifetime of failure; that's what they said when she tried to talk about it – they being family, friends, her psychiatrist. They said everyone suffered in their childhood.

Another Nurse Ratchet. The small, silent one from Manila leant down to Tessa on the floor. "Take." In one hand, a small plastic cup; in the other, one of paper with concertina sides.

She swallowed the pill and chased it with the water. "Can I get tea?"

"I bring it to you."

That was fine. She didn't feel like walking the corridor anyway. Her room, like her thoughts, encased her.

She'd had to make it all right, not just the event, but the aftermath when nothing happened and no one said anything at all. She remembered her burst into yellow light, the kitchen bright, her mother at the counter chopping carrots, the dog expectant at her feet. *They made me eat them* and her mother, without stopping, *Wash your hands.* At supper, her sisters, *They weren't real* and *It was only one,* and her father, *Dear, dear.* Oh, how they'd laughed. A funny family story. Ha ha.

A week ago, Freddy was crouched at the top of the stairs, his face pressed against the banisters. A week ago, Scott was shouting and the police were holding her down. The police car that had tailed her, the zebra running into the trees, the CIA waiting by the hat stand. The only thing to do was attack the house; destroy the kitchen, turn over the bathroom, throw everything in water. She'd tried to change it all around, get rid of the suffocating walls, but they'd stopped her. She knew it was them making the drawings change, the builders cancel, the architect put down the phone. She'd played it very cool on the journey in. Very cool. She knew the drill.

The stink of institution, Nurse Ratchet held Tessa's arm, shuffle, shuffle down the corridor to another room of single bed, locked window, a desk at which to write contrition. A cup of tepid Chamomile tea. She sat on the bed, her hands tucked between her legs.

The first time she'd had an episode, it had been a relief – an immeasurable gasp of air that had filled her lungs and made sense of the shouting, as if up to that point she'd been holding her breath. When she was twenty-one, they'd called it manic depression. She'd been at Manchester University. The Hacienda had reopened, the city was shot through with life and the drugs were plentiful: ecstasy, acid, speed, anything you wanted, as much as you wanted, and cheap like the clubs and the cider in the student bar. She hadn't been sleeping, she hadn't been working much either, essays half done and finished on the bus, late to lectures, tutorials missed; she'd been called in to see her tutor twice. But she didn't care; it was only her first year and she was having too much fun. Except she couldn't sleep.

To begin with, it was just after parties and who could sleep then anyway, with amphetamines coursing their veins? They all smoked a lot of pot to bring them down, but it did the opposite to Tessa. It charged her up. One night of no sleep was okay – she could handle that. But then it became two, then three in a row, and she'd be so wired she couldn't see straight. She went to the doctor for sleeping pills, he gave her enough for a week, *to reset her body clock,* but after they ran out, she was worse. Her brain wouldn't shut up, her jaw ached and she was frightened to go out.

It was Clare who persuaded her to see the doctor again, Clare who'd she'd met in her first week at university, both on acid they'd found themselves in an airlock between entrance hall and corridors and laughed till they'd peed, instantly friends. This time, the doctor said she might think about going home for a while, he could write to her tutor. He said she was suffering from stress.

Was that the word for it, when every minute of the day her thoughts told her she was in danger? All she wanted was to lie down, to make the noise stop, but it never stopped, it never shut up, it followed her everywhere. That's when the lists began. Writing down a strategy was the only moment of quiet. *Tidy desk, write essay, write out timetable, shop, food, hair,* but as the lists got longer, the panic rose and she'd screw them up, and the suffocation would be back, the stultifying immobilisation, the couldn't breathe. She had visions of earthquakes, buildings collapsing, children being crushed, her own hand disappearing under rubble.

She'd left before the end of term; she'd taken the train south. At King's Cross, she was followed by a man in a hat. She lost him on the tube, but at Victoria he reappeared in *Next* where she'd gone to buy a straw Stetson – better to disguise herself. He got on her train, and the chill sense that she was hunted followed her all the way to her parents' house. They lived in West Sussex then, they were yet to move to the sunshine of southern Spain. Theirs was a white cottage on the village green with a neat garden, low-beamed rooms, a bright, sunny kitchen and a cupboard under the stairs.

The chill was there as she got off the train, as she searched the platform for her father, there as she put her bag down in the hall. Everything was wrong. It was moving too fast. Her childhood room was different. Someone had changed the placement of her things in little incremental ways that only she could see.

"Lunch," her mother called up the stairs.

Perhaps if she rearranged everything.

"Lunch, Tessa," her mother shouted louder.

In the kitchen, cold beef salad and crushed potatoes with chives. Her mother wiping her hands. Her father with a gin and tonic. Sunshine, tiled floor, scrunched-up floral blinds, the dog scrabbling about his bowl, his nails clicking when he trotted over to greet her. Tessa put her hand down and scratched his head. She hoped her face was as bright as the surfaces, the sunshine, the ice in her father's glass.

"Just have the salad." Her mother moved the potatoes out of reach.

They'd taken her away after she ran at her mother with a kitchen knife.

"Where did it come from?" Her mother leaned forward; the psychiatrist leaned back. Tessa noticed how her mother's neat behind hardly touched the chair in the communal sitting room of The Priory, as if the place could infect her.

A month in that white castle in Richmond where ravens gathered on the ramparts and the richly painted rooms made you wonder what fairy tale you'd landed in. A month of sedatives and group therapy and climbing out of her window with new friends. They found magic mushrooms growing in the garden. When her mother came to take her home, she said, *I do hope you'll listen to the doctors and take more care of yourself now.* As if everything that had happened had been Tessa's fault. As if she'd been too sloppy with herself.

"Think of it like diabetes." The psychiatrist had lent her elbows on the desk. "You'd take insulin, wouldn't you? That's all they are, an adjustment to your chemistry. Your brain's misfiring. If we get you on the right dose, you can lead a normal life."

But what did they know about normal? What did anyone know?

"Accepting you have an illness is the first step."

Did that woman with the neat brown eyes and neat brown hair, and cardigan and pearls really think she knew the road better than Tessa?

"It's a propensity. We don't really know what sets it off in some people and not in others," the psychiatrist had explained to Tessa's mother. "Perhaps there's a history in the family...?" Her mother had let the question lift away on the warm summer air that had drifted in through the open windows. "Or simply puberty, the onset of hormones," continued the psychiatrist hurriedly, "pregnancy, drugs, a traumatic event..."

Tessa had thrown her flowered teacup across the room.

They'd called it a chemical imbalance and she'd tried to agree. She'd taken her pills and let them lean their full weight upon the door. They'd told her to forget the thoughts that possessed her, to ignore the incessant banging. They'd said her brain was a broken thing. But it wasn't her brain, it was the hinges, the lock, the six-year-old girl in meltdown. She kept pushing that cupboard door open, trying to burst out; the lock, the hinges weakened with every escape, and as the years passed and she'd gone from university, to job, to marriage, she'd found that to kick it open was the only way to feel alive.

The pill kicked in about the same time she decided she was getting bored. Shuffle, shuffle to the patients' lounge, Ethel by the kitchen hatch, arguing about sugar. String around her cardigan, a skirt too long, an effort given up. *That's me*, thought Tessa. *That's me twenty years from now.* By the window was Carrie, an elfin girl who talked to no one, and in the armchairs were Derek and Clive, who treated the place like a retreat. The first thing Clive had said when she'd met them was: *We're not the real Derek and Clive.* And Derek had said: *We just happen to be called Derek and Clive.*

"Good times," said Clive to no one in particular. He'd been in and out of institutions since he was seven. It was amazing what you could learn in a week, how open they were with each other. If only the psychiatrists knew.

"We heard you had a party," said Derek.

She'd imagined all sorts of things for her life, sat with clear intentions, done ceremonies; there were subtle altars all over her house, places she'd put special objects, a stone, a flower, a card, places where she'd lit incense and candles, where she'd wished and believed and thought, *Careful what you wish for,* while trying to hold the line between humility and power. She didn't understand any of it. She'd found a therapist who said, *You are held,* and banged a drum while tapping Tessa on the head. She'd stopped going after Scott had drawn the line at singing bowls. *Maybe you should try clearing up once in a while,* he'd snapped and she'd chucked the wooden mallet in the bin. The only thing holding Tessa right now were 1200mgs of Amisulpride and this chair, which made her itch.

Clive farted and Derek said, "Your health."

She flicked through an old magazine. Maybe it really was 2001. It was hard to tell.

"Someone to see you, Tessa," said Nurse Ratchet from the doorway.

"I'm busy."

"Not so busy as to see a friend, now, are you? Don't be silly."

Yes, that's what she was. Silly.

She didn't recognise her at first. If Clive hadn't pointed and said, "Um, um, you know, *EastEnders*, no, no, *Casualty. Casualty!*" she might not have placed her at all.

7 FIRST REHEARSAL

The cast jostled about her. Rehearsals went like a dream. At the pub, Brian said, "Why don't you direct? I could do with a break." Lights, action, applause. The whole of Midhurst loved her. Next year, they'd do Pinter.

Ros had been so lost in her daydream, she'd almost hit a woman scurrying across the car park at St Richards. She wouldn't mind directing. He only had to ask. She wrapped her coat around her and scurried like the woman against the biting cold, following signposts to Mercury Ward, a separate building from the main hospital, brick and square; this is what friends did, they visited each other in fuck-awful places. She'd dressed down for the occasion, she didn't want to stand out, her oldest jeans, trainers, a sweatshirt, her hair scraped up into a ponytail, she'd never been to a psychiatric ward before. In the antechamber of mental illness, a cork board chequered with green elastic holding pamphlets for Pilates and MIND, she waited for a small nurse with helmet-black hair to open the next set of doors and show her in. *I'm a friend,* she said to the question. The nurse led her down a corridor, *She'll be happy to see you,* and left her at the lounge of The Given Up – that's what they should have called it, like the day after the apocalypse when everyone was too tired to eat each other. Bodies everywhere. The stink of the place. Couldn't they open a window? All the closed-off atmosphere of hospital with added locks and there was Tessa, the collapsed heap of her, Ros touched her shoulder. "Hey, Tess."

The magazine in Tessa's hands fell to the floor. Ros had never seen her move so fast. Up and out of that chair, the two old blokes in the armchairs opposite laughing. The smaller, more revolting one in stained, ill-fitting trousers – the one who'd shouted, *EastEnders, no, no, Casualty!* – said, "You won't catch her."

Ros turned away from the sight of his belly, bursting without shame from the bottom of his lumberjack shirt. The other man laughed. Most people who recognised her asked her what *Nurse Fairhead* was like, but Tessa hadn't even made it to the doorway and they were already onto *Brexit*. Ros didn't know there were conversations in places like these. She'd imagined buckles and sadness and Tessa begging to be let out. She'd imagined gratitude. She chased her from stinking lounge to corridor of cheap doors and laminate signs – *Polite Notice. Abuse will not be tolerated* – and into a bedroom.

This time, she didn't touch her. "Tessa, it's me. Ros."

It was as if another person had stepped into Tessa's skin, someone demonic, large, and dead of eye, of erratic bursts of action.

"Sorry, Ros. Busy. I don't have time to see you now." She brushed her hair, sweep-sweep through the greasy, tangled locks. "Did you bring me my money?"

Ros wanted to do it for her. "Money?"

"Or cigarettes. Or phone. Did you bring me my phone? I told Scott to pack a bag."

"I didn't know I could bring anything. I will next time, though, if you like? I could bring you your things if you make a list."

"I need my other slippers."

"Slippers." Ros got out her phone.

"And cigarettes. And money."

"I did bring you this, though." She held out a copy of *Blithe Spirit*. She'd got it off Amazon.

"Don't forget my phone."

"I'll leave it on the bed, shall I?" She laid it gently on the cheap sheets. "I thought it would give you something to do, something to concentrate on. I've marked your lines." Ten minutes in that awful place and already she felt like she was dying. No wonder no one ever got better. She'd been planning on tea; she'd imagined a hug.

"I have to go out."

"Are you allowed out?"

"I have to go to the shops." Tessa barrelled past Ros and headed for the main door. At the entrance, she pointed at the large green button on the wall. "You have to press it."

"And also," Ros pressed the button. "Scott and Clare thought, I mean, we all thought, and it's only until you're better, that—"

The door buzzed. Tessa pushed it open.

"What I mean is, I just wanted to say not to worry. I'll keep your seat warm."

The airlock closed behind them. Tessa didn't seem to be listening. She held her bag in both hands pressed to her chest, her shapeless outfit. And she still had her slippers on.

"Tessa?" Ros wanted to get out, too. "Is there another button or something?"

"And if you're fucking him, I don't care."

"Excuse me?"

"I said if you're fucking him—"

They both heard the woosh of the doors behind them. Tessa's eyes flicked over Ros just once, briefly, as the two nurses grabbed her by the arms and hauled her back inside.

Ros didn't move. She waited for the airlock to close and pressed the button again. This time, the outside doors opened with a rush of air. Ros didn't look back.

She gunned her BMW away from St Richards, cutting off an ambulance as it pulled out of the drop-off bay. Fucking Scott? She undid her ponytail. God knows she'd been at that rodeo before. Forget Tessa, not forget, but don't worry, as worry wouldn't help anyone. What Tessa needed was support. They couldn't all go to pieces. It was important for Tessa's friends to stay strong and keep the ship afloat. First rehearsal was tonight. Tessa was just, she couldn't find the word, so she smoked a cigarette, grappling for her lighter as she took the turn for Midhurst. Tessa was just ill.

Ros left her discomfort on the A286. By the time she pulled up outside The South Downs Centre, the world was good again. Everything was fine. Tessa would get better, the show would go on, and Ros's ship wasn't just afloat, it was sailing. Who knew where this might lead?

She was bang on time. Brian would be thrilled. She slung her bag over her shoulder, pushed open the heavy doors and moved the green curtain aside. The hall was dusty and cavernous, high windows and chairs stacked against one wall. Brian at the far end was already laying out scripts on the stage.

"Ros! Come to keep an eye on us, have you?"

"Didn't Scott tell you?" She shoved off her coat, pulled

a chair from the stack and draped it over the back. She was sure the waft of Mercury Ward came with her.

"Tell me what?"

Ros picked up a script. It had *TESSA* written in the top-right corner. Beside the scripts was a new box of highlighters. Ros chose pink.

"Tell me what?" said Brian again, this time looking at his watch.

The door banged, the curtain moved aside and into the hall swept Diane, trailed by Issy, dragging her school satchel.

"Sorry, sorry," Diane's scarf wafted behind her. Issy almost trod on it.

"Pick up your bag," said Ros.

Next came Scott, Clare, and a stout woman in tweed. Ros put her script down and hugged Scott.

"Have you met our Mrs Bradman?" said Clare.

"Barbara." The stout woman in tweed held out her hand. "I saw you in *Casualty*."

"Tess not with you?" said Brian. He picked up the script Ros had left on the chair.

Scott took off his jacket. Pine needles fell onto the parquet floor. "She's in Spain. Sorry, Brian, should have rung you."

"Spain?" asked Brian.

"Parents," said Clare and Ros together.

"Ros is stepping in," said Clare. "Just until she's back."

Ros smiled at Brian.

"You could let her do the warm-ups," added Clare. Her Barbour left a scattering of straw. There was binding twine escaping from a hole in one of the pockets.

"Brian makes us do sit-ups," said Diane.

"For the stomach muscles," said Brian.

"I'm not lying on that floor," said Barbara.

"I'm sure I've forgotten everything," said Ros, stepping onto the stage.

She got them on their backs in a circle, feet to the centre, hands on their bellies, all except Issy, who refused.

"Now," said Ros, lying between Clare and Scott, "close your eyes and feel your bellies moving with your breath. Up, down, up, down, in, out, in, out."

"Do the hokey-cokey?" said Scott. Clare laughed.

"Eyes closed please, Scott. I want you to connect with your breath. It'll help with projecting. When you project your voice, it has to come from the diaphragm. We want the people at the back of the theatre to hear as well as the people in the front row, don't we?" The stage was cold and hard. She could feel Scott's warmth beside her.

"We rather want them to see the play, too," said Diane.

"I'm not sure I can get up," said Barbara.

"Can Mrs Bradman play her part lying down?" asked Scott.

"I don't think we're supposed to be talking," said Brian from the other side of the circle.

"I have to be back by eight." Barbara flashed a view of her undercarriage as she struggled to her feet.

"How about a few voice warm-ups?" said Brian, getting to his knees.

"Okay, if everyone wants to stand up," said Ros, standing, too. "Now, if we all take a space," she held her arms out, "like this. Find your space."

She saw Clare and Diane exchange a look. "And drop your arms, hands to bellies, ma-ma-ma-ma-maa, copy me."

"Mamma Mia!" shouted Issy in a song-song voice. "Here we go again."

Diane barked a laugh.

"Thank you, Issy," said Ros.

"Maybe that will do," said Brian.

"I can hand out exercises next week." Ros wiped the dust from her jeans. "They can practice at home."

Brian got down from the stage. "Come and get your scripts." He picked up his own as the others crowded round.

"Do pass mine," said Barbara. Clare handed it to her and passed Diane hers, too.

"And if you can all move to the side," Brian directed with his arms. "Issy, you too. Yes, that's right, up on the stage, stage left, please."

He pointed stage right, but Ros didn't bother to correct him. She stood beside Scott, waiting for Brian to decide if Diane should be sitting down or leaning on the mantelpiece. If they didn't want to know, that was their look-out. She was only trying to help.

"How's Freddy?" she whispered.

"Fine. Fine."

"And you?"

"Oh, you know."

"Why don't I come over one evening, do Freddy's tea, or something? My girls can look after themselves. It would give you a night off." There was no point in telling him. Tessa would probably forget, anyway. Some things were best left to sink.

"Ros? Scott? Can I see you in starting position?" called Brian. "Scott, there, there'll be a sofa there. And, Ros, we don't need you until Act Two. Come and take a pew." He patted the back of the chair that Issy had been sitting in.

"You mean, Scene Two," said Ros.

"We're going from the top," said Brian.

"You know, that would actually be great, if you could," said Scott, quietly.

"No problem, of course I could."

Ros bumped his arm gently as they parted.

8   JUST CASUAL

She arrived at Scott's house to find chaos. It was just gone six in the evening and she wished she'd got there sooner. Washing spread from utility to kitchen, the sink was piled with crockery, cutlery slid from the draining board and last night's supper was encrusted on pans on the stove. In among it all was Freddy, doing his homework.

"Where's your dad?" Ros had let herself in the back door. No one seemed to lock their houses round there.

Freddy shrugged. Ros put the shopping down and took off her coat. She hung it on the coat stand in the hall.

"I'm here." A hammering of feet, Scott's voice, and then Scott. "Sorry, Ros. A bit behind. Barbara was supposed to come this afternoon." He looked hopelessly at the mess.

"Not a problem, Scott. You go and have a nice time. Fred and I will manage."

"I'll clean up later."

"Don't you worry about it," said Ros.

"Freddy," said Freddy.

Scott kissed his son's head. "He doesn't like anyone calling him Fred except me and his mam."

"Freddy, it is." She smiled at the blond boy at the table, green eyes like his dad.

"You know where everything is? Fred. Be good. He has to finish his homework before Nintendo." Scott searched for his jacket and found it beneath her coat. "I'll be back by nine? That okay? Thanks so much. You're an angel."

"My pleasure." She leant against the sink. When she heard his car driving away, she started on the washing-up.

It was true, that in the early days of being a wife she'd had this feeling, and that within less than a year that feeling had turned to hate. It was true that she'd loved being a wife once or had felt the accoutrements to love that had made, in the opening gambit of marriage, housekeeping a pleasure not a chore. There was something satisfying about it, she thought now, moving about Scott's kitchen, the trails of him everywhere.

She put Freddy's supper in the oven and started on the laundry.

"Can I go on Nintendo?"

"Have you finished?" She switched on a white wash and ran a cloth over the counter above the machine, knocking grains of *Surf* onto the linoleum floor.

Freddy nodded.

"Off you go, then. Dinner in half an hour."

She smoked a cigarette, leaning in the open doorway to the garden, her coat over her shoulders. So this was Tessa's life. It didn't seem so bad.

*

Scott was only half an hour later than he'd said he'd be. It had given her the chance to light the fire and put on another wash.

He came clattering in with a blast of night air, smelling of the pub. "Sorry. Got waylaid."

Ros had a dishcloth over her shoulder. She dried her hands on it and hung it on the Aga. The kitchen sparkled; the draining board shone, the sink was empty, the surfaces wiped, the floor swept clean while from the utility room came the soothing rumble of the washing machine. Ros checked the oven, shook the carrots and got butter out of the fridge. "I thought you might be hungry." She put his supper down in front of him. "Will you have a glass of wine?" She sounded like him, that Irish arrangement of sentences that made everything soft. At LAMDA, they'd called her the lyrebird.

"What about you?"

"I ate earlier." She'd eaten Freddy's leftovers. She put on her coat.

"Where are you going?" He dug into his chicken. Garlic butter burst onto the plate.

"I thought I'd leave you in peace."

"Don't be stupid, Ros." He pushed the corkscrew toward her that she'd left on the table. She put down her bag. She'd bought the bottle at Waitrose; she'd guessed South African red.

"Did Barbara turn up?"

"She rang. I hope you don't mind, I answered it. She said something about her veins."

"You didn't do all this yourself now, did you, Ros?"

"No, the fairies did it. Of course I did. It was no bother. We don't want our Mrs Bradman collapsing on us." She was going to say *as well* but stopped herself.

"I'm not sure we'd have been any worse. Brian said he'd half a mind to put her in a barrow and wheel her about the stage. Might get her moving." He'd demolished his chicken and chips in the time it had taken Ros to take off her coat, open the bottle and pour two glasses; only a few carrots remained on his plate. He wiped them through the last of the garlic butter. "Fuck me, that was good. Didn't know I was so hungry. You can come round and cook any time." He turned his chair out from the table and crossed his legs. He still had his work boots on.

"You know, I'm really happy to, Scott. I mean it. The girls don't need me. They can always go round to Peter's. It's nice to have company."

"I don't mind the quiet."

She'd meant for her.

"Did Fred eat up? Was he no trouble?"

"No trouble. Is he doing okay?" Even pointing at Tessa felt delicate. "Does he ask about what happened?" She wanted to say *her*.

"He's a resilient lad. And it's not like it came out of the blue."

"I thought Clare said he was only little before."

"She's hardly super normal the rest of the time. How the kitchen was when you turned up is not a million miles away from how it normally is."

"Oh."

"She's not big on housekeeping."

"But she's very loving."

"She is that."

"And she is his mum. He must be missing her."

"It's a lot easier without her here." Scott refilled his glass. "Sorry." He looked at her across the silence. "You must think I'm a right cunt. She loves her son, but love doesn't do the washing-up, you know? Love doesn't make her a good mother. It's weird because when she's in hospital she's like the most nuts, but also the most honest. She gives in to it. She stops trying."

"Do you take him to visit her?"

"I'd have to be fucking mad to." Scott rubbed his face. "It would traumatise the lad. No one needs to see that. I only go because I have to. Only a masochist would want to visit. Or a fantasist."

"I'm thinking of having a dinner party." She hadn't been.

"Are you now?"

"For my birthday." She'd been planning on a spa at Lythe Hill.

"Twenty-one again, is it?"

"Just casual."

"I won't get my dinner suit out then, will I?" He leaned back, his hands clasped over his belly. There was nothing ugly and protruding about that stomach; it didn't spill out from his shirt and assault her eyes. It was flat, muscular. She assumed it was muscular. She finished her glass and pushed it away. It wouldn't do to stay too long.

"Don't get up." It didn't look like he was going to, but she said it anyway. She wasn't sure if he replied, maybe he mumbled something. He'd closed his eyes and she was too busy closing the door.

*

The next day, she met Clare for a walk. Wrapped in coats and scarves, the two women, one tall, the other short, set off through the park with Clare's terrier yapping at the legs of Crosby and Nash. Ros's Barbour was only a year old, but Clare's was torn at the hem and elbow, creased from being flung on,

61

ridden in and used as a dog bed when she hadn't anything else to hand. Bailing twine and straw escaped the pockets. Ros knew there was a knife in there, too – she'd seen Clare whip it out when she'd got her jeans caught on barbed wire the time she'd tried to vault over a fence. Today, a noseband was half-falling out, dropped in beside Clare's phone as if she didn't care, or didn't remember it would be forever getting stuck with grit. For Clare's birthday last spring, she'd given her a swanky new pig-skin phone case, but Clare didn't use it. She'd said she'd only ruin it and Ros had been embarrassed that she hadn't understood the rules, that no one gave presents like that round there. Clare had invited her to drinks at a wine bar in Midhurst, Ros had turned up with the present wrapped and bowed, Clare had looked surprised, and Ros had said, *Oh, it's nothing really,* and had so many vodkas she'd danced on the table.

"Ben-Ben." Clare's terrier was heading for the rabbit holes. The first time Ros had heard Clare call her dog's name she'd lost track of what she was saying. Then she'd gone home and put on a song she hadn't listened to in years. Then she'd got drunk.

She whistled for Crosby and Nash, who were fast disappearing over the next rise. She'd been planning on Stills and Young, too, until Peter had said, *Have you lost your mind?* They were so sweet as puppies. Now enormous and out of control, they ignored her. "I was thinking of having a few people over tomorrow, for my birthday, if you're not doing anything."

"Your birthday? Oh, Ros, you should have said."

"I am saying."

"No, but I mean – I'd love to come."

"Bring Nancy, if you like. Molly'll be sulking anyway. They may as well get the hump together."

"I thought you were getting on fine."

"We are. Just normal teenage stuff. If you could bring a whip, or whatever you use on a bloody difficult pony who won't shut up about how I'm ruining her life, then you could sort Issy out, too."

"A choke chain." Clare laughed. "Or maybe I could put her in a martingale and gag."

The reference was lost on Ros. She'd never had much interest in anything that involved opening her legs for no reason.

"She's doing great in the play," said Clare.

"That's how I'm ruining her life, apparently."

The dogs reappeared, hurtling towards them. Nash had a pheasant in his mouth. "Shit," said Ros. "Nashy, Nash-nash, come here. Come *here.*" The dog bounded past, followed by Crosby and Ben. "That's the third one he's caught this week."

"You might want to think about gun dog training," said Clare, walking quickly.

Up ahead, the dogs gathered by the wall. Ros chucked the dead pheasant into the bushes and snapped a lead on Crosby. "Don't tell Brian about dinner, will you?"

Clare took Ben's lead from around her neck. "Why would I tell Brian? I never see him outside of rehearsals, anyway."

"I thought he was always hanging around the stables."

"He delivers bedding, but he did that last week, and they're not shooting till next week."

They reached the gate and Clare opened it, Ben on his lead. Ros made a grab at Nash's collar, but he slipped through her legs and ran for the house.

"Just casual?" said Clare.

"Totally casual. About eight, that okay?"

"Sure." Clare opened the boot of her Subaru.

But nothing was casual for Ros.

As soon as Clare was out of sight, she shut the dogs in the utility room and set off for Waitrose, changed her mind and headed for the Cowdray Farm Shop. Beef Wellington. Too fussy. Sausages and mash. Too low-key. A whole salmon. But it was late autumn. Maybe smoked salmon to start, followed by fish pie. Too fishy. Vol-au-vent nibbles – she could go full Abigail's Party. Vol-au-vent with cocktails, smoked salmon on rye followed by Beef Wellington ready-made from the butcher at Cowdray. Irony, followed by simplicity, followed by show-off – perfect.

At the counter, she bumped into Brian.

"Elvira!" Ever since the start of rehearsals, he insisted on calling her that.

"Hello, Dr Bradman." She played along. It was easier.

"I see you're buying my beef."

"Is it yours? How lovely."

The butcher waited for her to choose which size she wanted; large or very large.

"Having a party?" said Brian.

"How many are you feeding, ma'am?" asked the butcher.

"Oh, I'm not sure." She smiled across the counter. "Let me count."

"What's the occasion?" said Brian.

"I was thinking of the Wellington." She glanced at the two Beef Wellingtons sat snug in a forest of fake greenery.

"Not sure who does those. Who does those, Simon?" Brian asked the butcher. "No," he held up his hand, "don't tell me." He leaned toward Ros. "Better to do it yourself."

"Oh God, far too complicated," said Ros, laughing.

"Special occasion, is it? Want to get it right?"

"My birthday, actually."

"Your birthday! Well now, how lovely. Either of those will be good. I can tell you their names if you like. That was Reg," he pointed, "and the other was Frank."

"No, don't!" She pushed him, playfully. The butcher waited.

"On hot for half an hour and then turn it down to 120," said Brian. "Gang going to be there?"

"How many will that one feed?" She pointed at the smaller of the two.

"Seven," said the butcher. "Six, if they're hungry."

"You'll want the bigger one," said Brian.

"Do you think?"

"Hungry lot."

"You must join us," said Ros.

"I'd be delighted." Brian stuck his hands in his pockets.

"The other one," she said to the butcher.

9　　　　　　　　　A BASTARD EX

It was the way Ros moved that had got her first. The way she sashayed about as if completely in control of her life, herself, her glorious body that even in her late forties hadn't lost the look of a thirty-year-old. Clare opened her front door, felt for the light, stumbled over a boot, chucked her keys on the kitchen table and put the kettle on. She felt like she'd been drunk from the minute she'd met her.

She wasn't drunk, not in that moment, though she felt like drinking. She'd waved goodbye to her vaguely, her hand out of the window as if she didn't care; they often walked their dogs together even though Clare's spaniel was on constant exercise at the yard, but Ros didn't need to know that. Whenever she texted, *Walk?* Clare would make out like that was a great idea. So that morning she'd done the same, *Sure* smiley face, even though she didn't have time. She'd left the mucking out, gone over to Ros's when she was supposed to be mending a stable door, parked outside her cottage, waited for Ros to put on her boots. She felt like an addict. Or a thief. She felt like she was betraying something. A couple of friends, out for a walk, *Just casual*, but nothing to do with Ros was casual for Clare. After she'd waved goodbye vaguely, pulled away slowly, as soon as the cottage and Ros were out of sight, she'd put her foot down and raced back to the stables to carry on shovelling horse shit and straw, before teaching a class of beginners and taking out two hacks. In the rain, she'd fixed the stable door that had lost its bolt, and in the tack room, electric heater on, jackets steaming, she'd interviewed a new stable girl, young and enthusiastic, prepared to work almost for free. Clare used to be like that, anything to be around horses, now it was anything to be around Ros.

Clare's kitchen was tiny, her cottage miniature, it was shoved on the end of the stable block like an afterthought. A two-up, two-down with a Raeburn that sometimes worked, a gas boiler that often didn't and creaky stairs to her bedroom with the floor that sloped one way, and Nancy's, which sloped the other. She threw her Barbour on the hooks by the warped front door, eased off her boots toe to heel, mud fell on the uneven cobbled floor as she picked up Nancy's Doc Martens and tidied both pairs onto the boot rack. The kettle hissed. She padded to the Raeburn in her socks and held out her freezing hands to the heat. It wasn't fair. Why did it have to be Ros? She put a potato in the oven, chopped the worst off the broccoli and turned on the water for a bath. Everything ached.

It was etched into her cells, the moment Ros had walked into Diane and Peter's enormous, well-lit kitchen, and Diane had said, "You must meet Peter's sister. She's just arrived. I want to introduce her to everyone." Diane had called out Ros's name, and from in among the red corduroy trousers and knee-length skirts, the dresses from Linea and suits from Hugo Boss, this beautiful dirty-blonde had turned around, smiled, walked over and held out her hand. It had been Christmas time then, too.

Clare stripped off her jumper and chucked it on a chair. Thinking of Ros always made her hot. She'd sweated through T-shirts for twelve months, gone for walks, met at the pub, come home stinking of something she couldn't have. For a year, she'd thought of nothing but her. All that she knew of her, she'd learnt from Ros herself: an actress, divorced, a bastard ex who used to hit her. Her brother had bought her a house to get her out of London. Legs that went on forever. A daughter who didn't eat. Another who didn't seem to like her much. A laugh that made Clare want to fuck her, a lack of inhibition among strangers and an aloofness up close that made Clare shiver and, mostly, especially, the thing that Clare knew worst of all about Ros was that Ros was in no way interested in her.

She took her tea to the tiny sitting room where she knelt on the settle and tried to light the fire. It hissed and spat, the kindling damp, but eventually a small flame gave way and Clare turned around, her back to it, and rested her cup on her knees. A two-seater sofa, its cover loose and faded green, a small and spindly rectangular table beside it was all the room could cope with, a door in the corner led upstairs. Nancy had stuck her artwork up on the rough white walls – she was obsessed with drawing hands. Clare looked at her own and picked dirt from beneath her thumbnail. Ros was all about men, how could she not be? She played them like instruments, the touch of a string here, a stray note when least expected, a clash of cymbals and innuendo. She'd watched her sing a duet with Brian at that first Christmas party a year ago when Ros knew only Peter and Diane; such confidence that it had made some raise their eyebrows, but Clare had been transfixed. 'Baby, It's Cold Outside', given all the sexual gusto of a seedy Paris revue; an audience immediately, completely submerged, embarrassed and cheering. It had been Ros's opening fling at their society, a bullet shot among them, a fire bolt crackling with heat, a reason for some people to say, *Well, really,* and distance themselves. She'd watched Peter laugh and Diane mouth, *She's an actress,* and shake her head, but a divorcée who looked like that was never going to be invited to the dinner parties of fragile marrieds, and all marriages, it seemed to Clare, were fragile.

Clare, on the other hand, was safe. None of them had met Nancy's father, and her Caribbean blood made most of them white and saving; Nancy rolled her eyes, but Clare didn't correct their soft pity, the unconscious bias that assumed she'd been left in the lurch shut down other questions, too. She and Nancy were considered unusual enough without gay being thrown into the mix. Why should she explain? She didn't want people knowing her business. Their assumptions were their problem and Sussex society had got to know Clare as a single mum, private, hard-working, not interested in meeting someone – they drew their own conclusions as to why. Everyone approved of Brian being in love with her, and some with her refusal of him. It made her solid, trustworthy, nice. She'd taken the lease on the old stables and built a business. She and Nancy got along fine. Tessa had moved back a few years later; they'd both grown up in West Sussex but hadn't known each other then. It was at Manchester University that they'd found the connection and been friends ever since. Ros had said to her once, *You're so in. Everybody loves you,* and she remembered thinking, *Not you, though.*

She hauled herself upstairs and into the bathroom; an old claw-foot bath, stains from the overflow and a cold tap that was stiff. A chipped sink and red tiles on the windowsill patterned with cracks. She turned on the hot tap. Nancy was staying at Ros's tonight.

It had been a devil throw, that they had daughters the same age, and that those daughters would become such friends. It had brought Clare into contact with Ros in ways she couldn't have dreamt of on that first night in Peter and Diane's well-lit kitchen. It had made it more painful. Every time Ros touched her, she'd think, *Please don't.* Like when she'd fallen out of the wine bar on Clare's last birthday and Clare had helped her up, she'd leaned on her all the way to the taxi rank and fallen asleep on her lap. Clare had almost carried her into her house. She'd pulled out the sofa bed while Ros directed drunkenly from an armchair, pointing and laughing, and when it was ready, Ros had crawled into it instead of going to her own bed upstairs. Clare hadn't known what to do. She'd lain beside her not breathing, not touching, keeping as far and as curled as the uncomfortable mattress would allow, and woken, sometime later in the dark, to notice Ros had gone. The next morning, Ros was contrite and beautiful. They'd hung their heads over coffee and Ros had told her about Harold, finishing with, *God, it's so good to talk. What happened with yours?* and Clare had shaken her head and said, *Oh, it was a long time ago. We were too young,* which was half true. The other half was that Nancy's dad had been Clare's best friend, still was, sort of, though these days he was married and lived in London, and they saw each other less now that Nancy was grown, but one drunken night long ago, he'd said, *Maybe you just haven't met the right man,* and Clare had thought, *Maybe?* and tried it with him, just for a laugh, just to see, but no. No man was the right man. Nancy was a gift out of something she hadn't wanted twice. Men, with their bits and rough edges, men with their lack of knowledge. Her body wanted soft; her body wanted dark; her body wanted Ros.

She stripped off and climbed into a shallow bath of tepid water. Shivering, she splashed her face and rubbed the worst of the dirt from her arms and feet. No lingering for Clare, she stood dripping and grabbed a towel, aware she shouldn't be ashamed, yet she was. There'd been pashes at school, the intensity of feelings strung up in hormones that confused her. There'd been fumbles at parties, girls trying it out on each other with laughter. She'd had a girlfriend at Manchester that she'd kept quiet about, separate from her crowd; an on-off thing that had lasted a year or so. She'd been older than Clare, not a student, they'd met at a club, she worked behind the bar. In the end, she'd snapped at Clare, *What are you so afraid of?* and left her for someone else. Clare still hadn't answered the question. She'd told Tessa casually one day, as if it wasn't something hidden, and added just as casually, *It's not a secret; it's only that I want to keep it private.* But that wasn't the truth.

She ate her baked potato and broccoli in front of the fire, crouched on the settle again, the flames built up to give a lasting heat. Her dressing gown over her pyjamas, they were light blue with small flowers, a present from her daughter, her dressing gown, towelling and grey, was man's size and old. The time Ros had given her the pig-skin phone case and touched her face with the tips of her fingers, and Clare hadn't known where to look, how she'd pulled away as if she wasn't grateful. The time Ros had tried to vault a barbed wire fence and Clare had had to cut her free, reaching between her legs to unhook the barbs from her inner thigh. Was God joking? It had felt so. She gave her broccoli stalk to Ben, who curled at her feet. The thing about winter, she thought, as she put her plate in the sink and turned off the kitchen lights, was that you could go to bed at seven, which she did, putting up the fireguard and climbing the creaking stairs to her sloping room. She cleaned her teeth, rubbed Nivea into the dry pores of her skin. She'd been in Ros's bathroom and it was nothing like this; every ointment and toner under the sun, every cream for younger skin, and why shouldn't she be that kind of woman, attentive to every line? It paid off, it showed, Ros's skin was flawless except for the flaws that made her human. She'd asked Clare to check a mole on her neck last time she'd stayed over and it had almost made Clare faint.

Cold in bed, the sheets and duvet not yet warm, she turned off her bedside light and lay in the dark, her eyes open. All she could think about was Ros and her hand drifted between her legs as she thought of how Ros moved, how she laughed, how she looked at her. Even as she breathed, she knew it was never, even as she closed her eyes, she knew this was as close and as real as it would get. Sleep would find her after, and as she drifted off to calm, she wished Tessa would come home, dilute the three that had become two, the friendship that would not leave her alone.

10　FIRST REHEARSAL IN MERCURY WARD

How long had she been there? It was hard to tell. Mercury Ward was like finding yourself in a hotel you'd forgotten you'd come to. Days and nights trailed into one another like the patients in the lounge, one becoming very like the next and identical to the one before, faces the same, food the same, a menu to look forward to only 'til she saw it. Tessa didn't eat except for breakfast and lunch. At night, she smoked.

Scott had been in earlier – or was it yesterday? He'd finally remembered her slippers. He'd thrown a new packet of tobacco at her, too.

"And a lighter?"

"You can have mine." He'd taken it out of his pocket.

She'd felt so tired she was hardly able to keep her eyes open.

He'd sat in the chair. "Everyone sends their love."

"Which everyone?"

"Clare, Brian, Peter, Diane. Everyone."

"And Ros?"

"Yes, Ros, too. Of course, Ros."

So he was fucking her. Of course he was. She supposed it had started weeks ago; she'd known from the minute Ros had walked into the lounge and let her gorgeous hair fall forward as she'd leant down to touch Tessa's shoulder. Why else would she have come? No one else bothered. And now, seeing Scott's face, it was as if he'd come right out with it; an expression like he deserved better, like she'd brought this on herself. So she'd said nothing. She'd lain on her back like a saint in a catacomb, her arms crossed over her chest and ignored his breathing. She'd heard him leave. She'd heard the door click shut. It had started raining again. He'd probably called the police on purpose to get her out of the way. He'd probably planned it from the moment Ros had sashayed into their lives a year ago. Was it only a year? It felt like forever. That woman had taken over.

No one had listened, no one being Clare. Everyone had fawned like she was Christmas and birthday all come at once, everyone's favourite new person, *a breath of fresh air,* but she hadn't fooled Tessa, only a bit but not really, and only because she was famous, sort of, and knew a few famous people and always knew what to say and how to say it and made everyone feel like they were the only person that mattered. Except her. She always mattered most. Tessa hadn't wanted to do the Harvest Fair anyway, she'd always got it wrong, piled the alter with tins of beans when she was supposed to weave loaves or something. Ros had got Hugh Bonneville to read the service. He wasn't even religious. Clare had said, *Jealousy's a curse,* and Tessa had felt ashamed.

Rain spattered the window and Tessa got up and shuffled the corridors, a half-built human in leggings and dressing gown, unable to settle, her afternoon drifted like she did, from bedroom to bathroom to lounge. She loitered at the office to get a rise out of the nurses; they teased her for having a husband so handsome and she said, *You can have him,* making one of them squeal. It wasn't the first time. He'd fucked the doula when Freddy was small; a tense woman with soft hands who'd come to help, too old for Scott but she'd heard them laughing, he'd probably called the police on her that time, too. Well, two could play at that game. She was having an affair with the boy in the room next door. They'd spoken through the grill in the courtyard; she might even be pregnant already.

Tessa drifted to the lounge; it had grown dark outside, the smell of something boiled and something else left too long on a hotplate drifted up to meet her. Even the most afraid found their way into that communal room at night to eat and not eat; they were guests in a strange motel grown familiar from passing each other in corridors yet bereft of partners, children, friends and freedom, they gathered like debris in the tattered chairs and at the peeling tables, taking up something to keep their hands busy, pretending all the time to not know each other. Ethel, unwashed and unbrushed, a string around her cardigan, made piles of sugar on a table; the white granules tipped from pink packets she'd secreted away in her sagging pockets all day. Carrie, too young to have suffered so much, wandered in and out and in again, each time pausing by the window to look upon the dirty courtyard of cigarette butts and weeds. Roger played Patience. Derek and Clive owned the armchairs like thrones and passed wind and judgement across the room.

Tessa picked up a plastic jug from a table and poured the contents into the yucca plant. Dry earth floated to the top and trickled down the side of the pot. Freddy rushed her thoughts like the kitchen after school. She left the jug on the floor, joined Derek and Clive, picked up a magazine and flicked through it.

"What about this then?" asked Derek, easing something from under his backside. He held up a book.

"Where did you get that?" said Tessa.

"Bin."

"Have you been in my room?"

"Found it in the trash."

"You've been in my room."

"Saw it when they were about to chuck it out."

"It's got your name in it," said Clive.

"*For Tessa, love Ros. Come back to us, Elvira!*" Derek read aloud.

"It's not mine." Tessa went back to her magazine. Cilla Black explained how she'd cut down on saturated fat.

"*The scene is the living-room of the Condomine's house in Kent,*" read Derek. "*The room is light, attractive and comfortably furnished.*"

"Could be describing here," said Clive.

"*On the left, there are French windows…*"

Clive pointed at the plate glass.

"*…opening onto the garden…*"

"Perfect."

"*On the right is an open fireplace.*"

They both eyed the yucca plant.

"*At the back, there are double doors leading to the hall, the dining room, the stairs and the servants quarters.*" Derek glanced over his shoulder at the serving hatch and door to the kitchen. Clive laughed.

"*When the curtain rises, it is about eight o'clock,*" Derek checked his watch, "*on a summer evening. There is a wood fire burning because it is an English summer evening.*"

"It means it's cold," said Roger, turning over a queen of spades.

"*The doors are open…* blah blah blah… *curtains partially closed. Ah, Edith comes in from the hall* – who's going to play Edith?"

Carrie appeared and scurried to the window.

"Perfect," cried Clive, clapping his hands. "Fucking perfect. Carrie, you're it."

"I'm what?" Carrie gnawed her fingernail.

"We need a Ruth," said Derek. He turned the page. "Ruth-Edith-Ruth-Edith, and then Charles. Lots of Charles." He flicked further through the script. "That'll be me, I think."

"What about me?" asked Ethel, leaving her sugar and standing over Derek.

"Madam Arcati," said Derek.

Ethel returned happily to her sugar.

"You shouldn't go through my stuff," said Tessa.

"It says here that you're Elvira."

"I'm not Elvira."

"We need an Elvira."

"I'm not fucking dead."

"Ruth, then, be Ruth. Clive will be Elvira."

"Suits me," said Clive.

"Noël Coward didn't approve of cross-dressing," said Roger.

"Knew him, did you?" said Clive.

"Saw a production in Eastbourne," said Roger. "You need a Dr Bradman."

"And a Mrs Bradman. You can be both Roger."

"Perfect for a schitzo," shouted Ethel.

"I'm Dissociative Identity Disorder," said Roger, leaning hard on each word.

"Schitzo," said Ethel.

"We don't use such words now, do we, Ethel," said Nurse Ratchet, crossing the lounge with a tray. On it were six small plastic Petri dishes holding pills in varying quantities, shapes and sizes. Beside them were paper cups, like cheap shot glasses, half-filled with water, their sides concertinaed into pleats.

"What's it about?" asked Carrie, chewing another nail.

"It's about a dead wife and a live wife and a man who sees things," said Roger.

"Like Derek," said Clive.

"It's about a woman who takes over," said Tessa.

"Isn't it about sightseeing?" said Ethel.

"You mean soothsaying," said Clive.

"You're going to hold a seance," said Derek.

"Now, now." Nurse Ratchet whipped the script out of Derek's hands. "We'll have none of that, thank you."

"Come on, Tracy, don't be a spoilsport. Give it back."

"Have you had it passed?"

"Derek shat a script!" shouted Ethel.

"I found it in the bin," said Derek.

"We'll see about that." Nurse Ratchet slipped it into the large front pocket of her tabard.

"Come on," said Derek. "Give it back. What else have we got to do?"

"It was a hit in '41," said Roger.

"He was there," said Clive.

"Were you?" asked Carrie.

"Stupid girl," said Roger.

"It's just a bit of fun, Tracy. Give it back."

"Dr Patel can decide in the morning." Nurse Ratchet held out a Petri dish and shot glass to Derek.

"I think I'll take the red pill tonight, Morpheus." Derek tipped the pill into his mouth and chased it with water.

Within half an hour, the lounge was quiet and everyone had gone to bed – Tessa to her single room in which to dream contrition. The sedative washed over her, the sense of it calming before the pill kicked in, she would sleep, and she would rest, and for ten blissful hours she would be somewhere else where she was well. This place that held her was a home of sorts, a family of like-minds; she knew the walls, the rules, the rivulets of time that would deliver her, half-baked back into the real world where her husband didn't love her anymore. She knew she was doomed.

The lights dimmed and the members of Mercury Ward slept, while ten miles away the party was just beginning. Clare stood in front of her bedroom mirror and wished she didn't see what she saw. Peter ironed his trousers while Diane ran a bath. Scott sniffed a shirt and threw it in the laundry basket. Brian rubbed pomade into his hair and combed it flat, as Ros, in her sweet little cottage on the edge of Petworth Park, put the Beef Wellington in the oven, looked at the clock, said, *Fuck it,* to no one in particular, and poured herself another cocktail. They'd all be there in half an hour. And it was her birthday. If anyone deserved a night off, it was her.

11

THE DINNER PARTY

Clare and Brian turned up together, Ros took the bottle out of Brian's hands.

"Thanks, Brian, decent of you. Get yourself a drink." She pointed through to the sitting room. "I need Clare's advice on the dauphinoise."

"Right-o." He went one way and Ros and Clare, the other.

"He literally turned up at my house," said Clare as soon as Brian was out of earshot. "Told me he thought I might want a lift. I didn't know what to do."

Ros put the bottle of Merlot on the countertop next to a packet of Loch Fyne salmon. "He probably sniffed his beef." She nodded towards the Aga.

The kitchen was crooked and sloping; Crosby and Nash got up to greet Clare with tails wagging and returned to their beds, tucked away on either side of the two-door Aga, which had been set in an old fireplace. Wattle and daub had been pulled away from dividing walls that no longer served a purpose in the modern, open-plan design of life, which valued light above warmth; some of the wooden framework was left, into which nails had been hammered to provide a casual place for aprons and cloth bags. The countertops and cupboards had been laminated in the sixties, the Belfast sink had no draining board and the uneven floor was bare cobbles.

"I feel terrible." Clare threw her coat into the utility room. It landed on the floor. "Should I ask him to go?"

Ros put her hand on Clare's arm. "No, no. No harm done. He just can't keep away from you, can he? Poor old Brian, lost in love. He must be lonely. We'll set another place."

"You're too kind," said Clare, moving a crackle-glazed platter on the kitchen table slightly to the left.

"Knock-knock," said Diane, sweeping in. "Evening, my darlings. Ros, take off that apron and give me a job. Where are the girls? They should be helping."

"Upstairs." Ros kept her apron on. To Clare, she said, "Where's Nance?"

Clare looked behind her. "Probably mid-text somewhere. You'd think they could wait five minutes. I thought she was following me."

"She's probably gone straight up to Moll's room," said Ros.

"Smells delicious," said Diane. "What do you want done with this salmon?" She picked it up and inspected it.

Ros took it out of Diane's hands. "We're having *gravadlax*." She crouched over the shopping bags, which she'd only half-emptied, and pulled out a packet of rye bread rounds. "Can you make a little arrangement on each? The sauce is somewhere." She rootled further and brought out a jar with curly writing on the label. "And dill is up there." She pointed at the windowsill above the sink. Somewhere between bumping into Brian and finishing her shop she'd given up on vol-au-vents. She'd spent all afternoon making the dauphinoise. By her second negroni, she hadn't cared anymore that it looked nothing like Nigel Slater's.

Diane settled down at the table with a pair of scissors. "Such a lovely way to start a meal, I always think. So refreshing."

Ros put the fresh dill beside her. "It's for nibbles with drinks. We're not having a starter."

"Oh," said Diane.

Ros ignored her. No one ever ate at dinner parties.

"I'll set another place." Clare opened drawers and shut them again.

"Is Tessa coming?" asked Diane.

"For Brian," said Clare.

"Cutlery on the left." Ros pointed at the drawers by the kettle.

"No news is bad news, is it, then?" Diane looked around at Clare and Ros. Ros unscrewed the cap of Brian's wine, and Clare picked out a knife and fork. Diane said, "Don't worry. I know perfectly well where she is. Peter saw Scott at rugby."

With a knife, fork and spoon bunched in her hands, Clare said, "Which napkins are you using?"

"I don't know why it's such a secret," continued Diane as she scissored up the smoked salmon. Her usual scarf abandoned for three strings of pearls, she'd adorned her wrists with so many silver bangles they went halfway up her forearms and clanged against the edge of the plate.

"Some things are just private, aren't they?" said Ros, handing Clare a paper napkin with *Happy Christmas* scrawled across it.

"Poor Tessa," said Diane.

"Spanish still got her?" said Brian, appearing suddenly in

the kitchen doorway, a glass of whisky in his hand. He filled the small kitchen with tweed.

Ros threw Diane a look. To Brian, she said, "What can I get you?"

"Ice." He swirled his glass.

"Why don't you go and sit by the fire? Clare will bring you some, won't you, Clare?"

Clare was crouched at the small, wonky dresser trying to lever out a dinner plate from beneath a stack of side plates. She made a face only Ros could see.

Ros took a Thomas the Tank Engine place mat from the dresser drawer above Clare's head and ushered Brian through the low kitchen door into the sitting room of dark beams and leaking windows. The table she used as a desk she'd pulled away from the wall into the centre of the room and levered in the extra leaves to make it big enough. Her mother hadn't wanted it when she'd downsized to a flat in London. Peter had said she could have it. She'd already lit the candles in the silver candelabra and arranged either side of it a vase of loose flowers, the silver salt and pepper shakers, and a jug of water in case anyone forgot to drink. Eight place settings, each with an Alan Bennett *Talking Heads* place mat; she'd found the set in Jubilee Market that day she'd gone shopping with Ben for a present for Cara. Thora Hird, Maggie Smith, Eileen Atkins and Julie Walters, framed by mismatched silver cutlery, smiled up twice. They'd thought they were perfect, her and Ben, laughing in the dripping rain, trying to keep under the awning, but that birthday had been the night of the final row and Ros hadn't even got them out of her bag. Cara wouldn't have appreciated them, anyway. She'd already lost her sense of humour.

Nine chairs; she added the children's place mat for Brian

and moved the jug to the windowsill to make more room. The sofa was pushed under the window, but two armchairs still faced the fire. Peter was in one of them; Ros shooed Brian into the other. She returned to the kitchen, passing Clare in the doorway with a cup of ice.

"And you've not been to see her," Diane was saying, as Ros came back in.

"Evening, all." Scott arrived with a blast of outside air.

"Scotty!" said Ros.

"How are we all?" He held out a bottle and a card to Ros. "Bottle from me, card from Fred."

"Oh no, that's too sweet."

"He made it for you."

"That's too sweet of him," said Ros again. Blue paper folded in half, a red heart stuck on the front and *Happy Birthday Ros* written shakily on the inside in green felt tip, she propped it on the windowsill where it fell over.

"No," said Clare, coming back in. "Hey, Scott."

"Can I do anything?" asked Scott.

"Make us all cocktails," said Ros. "I'm on negronis."

Scott went off in search of Campari and Ros checked the beef.

*

The dauphinoise was stodgy, the Beef Wellington overcooked and the salad didn't really go with any of it, but it didn't matter. It was her birthday. Who cared? Alcohol took the place of most things and it did that night; the wine flowed and soon the table was a mass of ashtrays and laughter and rambling anecdotes, mostly from Brian, who'd taken the floor with stories of the army.

"Most life-threatening," he continued, in answer to a question Issy had asked about twenty minutes ago, before she'd got bored and gone to bed, "had to be Iraq. Knew a fella who liked playing chicken."

"Do you mean like in *Rebel Without a Cause*?" asked Nancy. She and Molly were into James Dean; they thought they'd discovered him. Nancy was small, like Clare, but with auburn curls and Caribbean skin; her mother's bones, her father's blood. When Ros had first met her, she'd thought, *Another piece of the jigsaw,* but Clare had remained mute. She'd never met anyone so private. Molly had said, *Maybe she just doesn't like talking about it,* and when Ros had pushed her, she'd snapped, *Nance talks to her dad all the time. It's fine. Clare's really cool,* and that had put an end to it.

"Not RPGs?" said Ros, grabbing the acronym from the news.

"The enemy's predictable," said Brian. "It's the ones inside the base you want to watch. Just because he's wearing the same uniform doesn't mean he's harmless. This fella, he held it against you if you said no. Wasn't right, to say no."

"Would you drive towards a cliff?" asked Molly.

"At each other," said Brian. "First one to brake."

"You'd think you'd want to do something quiet in your spare time," said Diane.

"Like crocheting," said Ros and everyone laughed except Molly, who looked annoyed. Ros motioned at Clare to pass the bottle. "Why don't you two girls get down?"

"Off to smoke pot," said Peter, after they'd gone.

"I found some in Molly's room," said Ros.

"I do hope you took it," said Diane.

"Obvs." Ros got up and fetched a little box from behind

a book on the shelves. "Who wants to roll?" And everyone laughed again.

Peter and Clare cleared the plates, Ros opened another bottle and Diane stoked the fire.

"What about you then, Scotto?" Brian passed the joint to Peter who handed it straight on to Diane. They were settled again at the table; clean plates, a cheeseboard and grapes, a plate of oatcakes, more wine. "You must have had a few," finished Brian, barely covering a belch.

"There was this one time in Harare. I'd just had the Land Rover painted."

"You did that yourself?" asked Ros.

"We had three of them."

"A fleet of zebras," said Ros. "How romantic."

"Not much romance to getting shot at," said Scott.

"What about lions?" asked Ros.

"They're not roaming the streets, Ros," said Peter. "Africa is somewhat more civilised than that."

"Africa is a continent," said Ros. "If you must be pedantic."

"Elephants, though," continued Scott. "Down south. Got charged a few times."

"See?" Ros stuck her tongue out at her brother and took the joint from Clare.

"Miss it," said Scott.

"Do you?" said Clare.

"Expect it was tough on the old bones," said Brian.

"Kept the bone rattler," said Scott.

"Can see you for miles," said Brian.

In each of their minds, Tessa loomed; Tessa perched high on the seat beside Scott, Tessa complaining how uncomfortable it was, Tessa in late summer, peasant sleeves and white jeans, climbing out of the zebra-striped truck.

"Any word from your wife?" said Brian.

"Cake!" shouted Ros. She'd completely forgotten the individual chocolate Rice Krispies she'd bought as a joke. She'd stuck each with a birthday candle.

"Save it for the girls," said Diane. Peter yawned and Diane patted his knee. "Time for bed, I think."

"I'm off, too," said Scott, finishing the joint.

Clare carried the untouched cheeseboard to the kitchen.

"Well, it's been lovely," said Brian, slapping both hands on his enormous thighs. "You ready?" he added to Clare as she came back in.

"You can stay here," said Ros, reaching lazily for her hand. "I'm sure Moll will want Nancy to stay."

"All girls together," said Brian. "Come on, then, Scotto. Let's leave them to it."

"Oh, do leave him, Brian. We'll get him up," said Ros.

Scott had fallen asleep in his chair, his arms crossed, his chin tucked to his chest.

"Not sure he should drive," said Brian.

"I'll make him coffee," said Ros, not moving.

"That'd be lovely." Brian sat down again.

Ros and Clare exchanged glances.

Clare said, "You know what, Brian, do you mind? Scott just needs five minutes. We'll only make him a shot. Not a whole pot and, you know, we're all a bit knackered, don't want to make too much noise. The girls'll be asleep."

"Girly chat, is it?" said Brian, heaving himself up again.

"Something like that." Clare smiled.

"You make sure he's fit to be behind a wheel." He motioned at Scott.

"Of course," said Ros. She put her feet up on the chair beside her.

After an espresso, and one more smoke for the road, Scott, roused by the door slamming after Brian, was ready to stand up. Ros stood shivering on the front steps as he went through his pockets for his keys. "Will I come and do Freddy's tea again this week?" There, that Irish syntax she couldn't help copying whenever she was near him. "That was so sweet of him to make me a card."

Scott squeezed his thumb and forefinger into the corners of his eyes and shook his head to wake himself. "He likes you. He says you make him laugh."

"You look like you could do with about fifteen nights off."

"There is that, too."

"How is she?"

"Oh," he shook his head again, "you know. It's hard, places like that, if you've never been."

"This Friday, then? Same time?"

"You're a sweetheart." He touched her face. "Happy birthday."

She closed the door and went upstairs in search of bedding. With a duvet over one arm and a pillow under the other, she took the stairs carefully. He shouldn't touch her like that. It wasn't fair. Clare had finished clearing the table and already pushed it against the wall to make room for the sofa bed. She was struggling with the hinge. Ros leaned down beside her, her hands on the ancient frame. She didn't know how many times she'd caught her fingers.

"Nightcap?" asked Clare, as the bed snapped flat.

12

ROS SEES HER ANALYST

"Passive-aggressive men are angry at their mothers."
Her analyst crossed his legs the other way. He wore beige
trousers. They annoyed her.

"That's Harold all over," replied Ros, upright in a large
red leather low-backed chair, the kind that tipped you into
its crevices and made it hard to feel in control. She always
had the urge to sit cross-legged in it, like a child, but she
always, too, wore a skirt when she came to London.

The room was sparse, not a comfortable place, no books
nor photographs, no sign of a personal life. Her analyst had
his desk to lean on; she had nothing. He didn't write much
in her file anymore. It was open on the desk, his notes of six
years placed neatly to the side. It would help if their chairs
were the same height.

She'd kicked off by complaining about another email
from Harold, saying he was taking the girls skiing.

"And how are you coping?"

Ros shrugged. "Okay, I suppose. Freddy gave me a
birthday card."

"Who's Freddy?"

"Scott's son. I've been babysitting. Helping out. His
wife's a friend of mine. She's in hospital."

"And her son gave you a birthday card?"

"Made, actually. It was really sweet."

Her analyst nodded. He was balding. That annoyed her, too.

"I don't know why I told you that. It was just that I thought it was sweet. It made me feel good."

"Did the girls give you anything?"

"Molly got me the *Peaky Blinders* box set and Issy made me a tea cosy, or a hat – it was hard to tell. I had friends round for dinner. It was fun."

"But your friend's son's card meant more to you?"

"I didn't say that."

"But you mentioned it first."

"Because it came to mind first, that's all." She sipped her coffee.

"She's a good friend, is she?"

"Sure. Her husband's in the play." Another sip.

"What part is he playing?"

"Opposite me, actually." She laughed. "My husband."

"And she's in hospital?"

"I'm just standing in for her." They'd spoken over each other. Ros ran her fingers through her hair. "In the play, I mean. I'm just standing in for her in the play. It's her part, so... anyway, it's fine." She crossed her legs the other way. "What I mean is, it's obviously not fine, she's had a breakdown, she has psychiatric problems, but I wanted her to have the script."

"In a psychiatric hospital?"

"I just thought it would be something to look forward to." She wished she'd never been. If Tessa said anything, she'd say she was making it up. "I didn't tell anyone."

"Why didn't you tell anyone?"

"Because you told me not to get involved in other people's business." She fiddled with the chin hair that had been irritating her since the waiting room.

"But she knows you're babysitting?"

Ros put her cup on the floor. "I don't see why I have to report every minute detail of everything I do to everyone. Anyway, nothing happened."

He raised his eyebrows. They were neat. "What happened?"

The same fucking thing as always. *If you're fucking him, I don't care...* Why couldn't she keep her head down? She was only trying to help. "Nothing. I told you. I don't think she even recognised me."

"Were you there last night?"

"At the hospital?"

"At her house."

Ros nodded.

"And how does that make you feel?"

"It's hard. He's my friend."

"I thought you said *she* was your friend." The gentleness of her analyst's voice made her want to hit him.

Ros picked up her cup again. "They're both my friend."

"Does he talk about his marriage with you?"

All last night, he'd talked about it. She hadn't got home till one. She looked at her knuckles. She'd grazed them on the wall trying to put Crosby's lead on. "It's funny to be acting again. I mean, good, good to be doing it again. Weird. But, you know, it's something isn't it? I mean it's not the Vaudeville, but I never thought I'd get the chance. Peter doesn't want me to. He keeps telling me to get a proper job. No such thing as a free roof. He thinks I should retrain."

"In what?"

"Anything." He'd suggested dog-walking. She'd retorted that she hardly needed training for that. He'd said, *Why don't you do it then?* She could hardly control her own dogs. That's why. He knew that. Her analyst looked at the clock and Ros did, too. Ten to three. Time played tricks on her here; there was always too much or too little.

Released to her car, she checked her face in the mirror, searching with her thumb for the chin hair. With the tweezers she kept in the car door, she plucked, and felt with her fingers for more. The rest of her looked okay. She ruffled her hair, snapped the sun visor back in place and pulled onto Westbourne Grove.

The city felt like an ex-lover who claimed he'd hadn't cared; the streets she knew so well carried on life without her. There, the school Molly had started at. There, the corner where Issy had lost her bike. That restaurant where Harold had taken her when she'd landed *Casualty.* The hair salon she'd gone to when Harold wouldn't take her back. She wound through Shepherd's Bush and swung left towards Hammersmith, grateful to leave it all behind. She and Harold had talked about moving to the country. They'd even driven down a few times, for weekends with Peter and Diane, but the thought of beginning again with him had been too much. She'd other plans back then. She'd believed in other things.

She resisted the urge to put on the music that would remind her. It would only make her sad. What a bastard he'd been. The whole thing had been one long fucking mess. Did they really think she'd make things up when there was so much to lose? Her best friend's husband was the last man on earth she'd have wanted to fall in love with her. It was him who'd seduced her, not the other way around. When she thought of the words he'd said to her, the hours they'd spent talking quietly off stage, gathering their things late at night, the bus rides home. She still had his texts and emails, the playlists she'd made. Jealous, that's what Cara had been. She'd had everything: the perfect man, the perfect marriage. The only thing Ros had been better at was getting pregnant.

The hint of rain that had hung heavy all day became a downpour as she drew up at the lights in Roehampton. She hadn't just lost her marriage, she'd lost her career and a goddaughter, too. It was Cara who'd encouraged her to take the part for Christ's sake, she'd said, *You'd be doing me a favour, Ros. It's just a play.* Just a play. Just *Three Sisters* at the Young Vic. Just the same play they'd done in their final year at LAMDA, the part of Masha that Cara had wanted all her life. She'd missed out to Ros once, she wasn't going through that again – joking, but not joking; they'd both gone up for it and Cara had got it. She'd come round and sat on the sofa, contrite but pleased, not hiding it. She'd said, *Sorry, I know you wanted it,* and Ros had replied, *I'm happy for you,* and she had been, of course she had. Harold had said, *Jump into her grave as quick, would you?* When, three weeks into rehearsals, Cara had backed out; Ros gripped the wheel. *Fuck him.* It wasn't her fault Cara's confidence had gone. When she'd said, *Are you sure you're up to it?,* she'd only been trying to protect her; she'd known how fragile her best friend was.

Encased in metal, the engine purring, the heating on, Ros felt safe and warm as her thoughts turned to Scott. Last night had been a deepening of something; she wished she could put her finger on it. He'd opened to her like a parched man given water. When she'd arrived at his house, with a lasagne from Cook, garlic bread from Waitrose and a packet of frozen peas, he'd said, *Would it be weird if I went and had a bath? Sorry, I should have called. I'm knackered, don't really feel like going out.* And she'd said, *Don't be ridiculous. I'm here to help. I'll get the dinner on.* Luckily, she'd brought enough for all of them. She'd busied about the kitchen while he'd gone off upstairs, a wipe of the cooker, a sweep of the floor, crumbs from the counter dropped into the palm of her hand and when he'd come down, feet bare, hair wet, he'd changed into sweatpants and jumper. Over dinner, she'd done impressions of Professor McGonagall and made Freddy peel with laughter, and after Scott had tucked his son up in bed, she'd stayed for another drink, and then another. When she'd finally looked at the clock, he'd said, *There's never a right time to leave,* and for a moment she'd thought he was talking about her. Poor Scott. She could see it in his eyes. She knew what trapped looked like.

She drew up outside the theatre with a screech, the windscreen wipers going full pelt and the tyres throwing cascades of dirty water. The same car she'd hauled baby seats in and out of, the same car in which she'd rowed with Harold for the last time. *Act normal,* she thought, running into rehearsals only half an hour late. It was what she'd told herself before.

13   DRESS REHEARSAL IN MERCURY WARD

Fourteen miles away in Mercury Ward, Tessa lay curled on her bed. The cheap, thin, poor excuse for a duvet hardly covered her. She'd forgotten what her bed at home felt like. She only knew a single mattress, a pillow with no depth. She sat up. It was cold and no weather to go outside, but she wrapped her coat around her dressing gown and, in slippered feet, went to the courtyard. The boy in the room next door had left, no voice at the grill when she whistled for him. If she was pregnant, they'd have to deal with it. Change her meds. With her fingers cupped over her roll-up as if it were a spliff, she smoked quickly in the rain. The glow of burning tobacco gave her comfort.

Fruit tea that went cold and stewed before she'd drunk it. Clive and Derek in the armchairs, Carrie by the window, Roger at the table, Ethel twisting string into a knot and arguing about milk at the hatch. There were new arrivals, too – a flurry of them over the past week. A full moon always sent the crazies crazy and psychiatric wards prepared for them, tossing science aside like air traffic controllers when Mercury went retrograde. This Mercury was in retrograde all the time. Mercury Ward was one long backward step into oblivion. She'd heard the nurses discussing doubling up on shifts.

Shuffle-shuffle to the office, the 400mgs of Olanzapine had sent her crashing. Tearing up your house was not okay, but a woman dying quietly inside apparently was. Keep your death to yourself, that was the message. She'd intentionally not brushed her hair.

"Tessa!" said Dr Patel, brightly. "And how are we?"

She wished healthcare professionals would have the decency to use correct personal pronouns. *We* weren't anything. "Fine."

Dr Patel looked at Tessa's notes. "I wonder if we shouldn't try you on something a little less heavy."

Like a concrete hat. That's what these drugs felt like. Like someone had come in the night and fitted a concrete hat to her head and poured lead into her feet.

"Do you feel you could cope with something lighter?"

Like a fedora? Or a Stetson? "I'd like to stay on longer."

"On Olanzapine?"

"I want to see a gynaecologist."

Dr Patel smiled.

"I mean an obstet... an obstret." She never could pronounce it. When she was pregnant with Freddy, they'd said she wasn't taking it seriously.

"Obstetrician?" corrected Dr Patel. She wore a shirt with small flowers on the collar. Tessa focused on them. Dr Patel adjusted her glasses. "Your son's ten, isn't he?"

Why did she have to mention Freddy? "I'm not ready to go home."

"I know this is distressing for you, Tessa. But you must fit yourself back into normal life if you want to get better."

But what if she didn't want to get better? What if the exaggerated highs and death-defying lows were all she'd got? "My husband doesn't want me home."

"Now, Tessa," Dr Patel looked at her watch. "That's simply not true. I've worked here a long time and no one gets more attention than you. He comes in every week, doesn't he? Didn't I see him yesterday? Some of our guests have no visitors at all."

He'd brought her a card from Freddy and she'd hidden behind the yucca until Clive had started making ghost noises and Ethel had turned over a chair. She'd only taken him to her room to stop Clive asking if he wanted to see Act Two. She'd told him she knew everything, there was no point in lying, but he hadn't wanted to talk about it. He hadn't wanted to talk about anything except when she was coming home and did she want more cigarettes.

"He said as far as he was concerned, you could come home any time."

He'd probably said, *She'll do anything to avoid getting up.* "I'm better with Zoloft."

"I don't think Sertraline is the thing."

But it was. She was depressed, not psychotic – why couldn't anyone see that? Who wouldn't lose their shit if nobody believed them? And antipsychotics were contra-indicated for pregnancy. Dr Patel should know that, but instead she closed her file, stood up and held the door for Tessa.

Shuffle-shuffle to the lounge where she found Derek moving chairs and Clive trying to convince Ethel to wear a tea towel on her head.

"Hold it under your chin, lie on the floor with your feet up and start screaming."

"Why do I have to scream?" said Ethel, twisting string through her fingers.

"Because you've seen a ghost." He flicked through the pages. "Yes, here, they've all come for dinner, they're having a seance and then you give a loud scream and fall off the stool onto the floor."

"She has to end up with her feet on the stool," said Roger.

Clive had a sheet wound over his clothes; it went around his waist and was tied in a knot over one shoulder. He swished about, trying it out. There was a stain where it bunched across his collarbone.

"Is it a Roman play?" asked Carrie.

"Stupid girl," said Roger.

"I told you it looked like a toga," said Derek. He'd turned a pillowcase into a cravat. "Tessa. There you are. You've missed scene one."

"I read for you," said Clive.

"I thought we weren't allowed," said Tessa. Her head hurt.

"Patel's calling it *drama therapy*. Evening performances only."

"Before cocktails," said Roger.

"You're on," said Derek to Clive. He pointed at the dying yucca. "Get thee behind the fireplace."

"How can he be behind a fireplace?" asked Tessa.

"Because he's a ghost," said Roger.

"Ready?" Derek tipped a table on its side, sending old copies of *National Geographic* and *TV Guide* fanning out onto the carpet. Richard and Judy smiled up from 1989. "Give me *perfectly strange and very charming.*"

"*Leave it where it is,*" said Clive, rustling the yucca leaves.

"You sound like you've been at the nitrous oxide," said Derek.

"Kenneth Williams," shouted Ethel from the floor.

"I saw him at the Almeida," said Roger.

"I'm not playing," said Tessa.

"Oh, come on, Tess," said Derek.

"We need you," said Clive.

"Let's get to a good bit," said Derek. "How about this: Elvira, you stay where you are. Dr Bradman, come and wake Madam Arcati."

"Am I supposed to be asleep?" said Ethel, kicking her legs in the air.

"Fainted," said Roger, irritably. "You've fainted."

"I can faint." Ethel closed her eyes, opened her mouth and flung her arms above her head. The armpit holes in her cardigan yawned.

"Charming," said Roger.

"What am I supposed to do?" asked Carrie from the window.

"Nothing," said Roger.

"Keep practising your curtsies," said Derek. He knelt beside Ethel and waved his hands near her shoulders. "Pretend I'm shaking you violently. *Wake up, Madam Arcati! Wake up!*"

Roger coughed. "*Here – go easy, old man!*"

"Surprisingly good," said Clive from behind the yucca.

"I played Richard III at the National," said Roger.

"Is that what tipped you over the edge?" Clive rustled the leaves again.

"You're not supposed to be talking," said Derek. "Tessa, you go and pretend to get Madam Arcati a brandy. Ethel? You can get up now. Go and sit in that armchair. Me and Dr Bradman will pretend to lift you."

"I'd rather not," said Roger.

"Just *pretend*," said Derek.

Tessa got a cup from the kitchen hatch. She gave it to Ethel, who smiled happily up at everyone from the deep, red, tattered chair that was usually Derek's.

"Move it along," said Clive. "Isn't it time for my entrance?"

"What about me?" asked Carrie from the window.

Derek sat down in Clive's armchair. "Okay. All right. Big entrance." He turned the pages. "Edith," he pointed at Carrie, without looking up, "you've done your bit, you can go."

"But I haven't done anything."

"You carried that tray beautifully," said Derek.

"She was supposed to run," said Roger.

"And Madam Arcati, you're off stage too. You were marvellous."

"Was I?"

"No," said Roger.

"Elvira, you need to get yourself over to the window – that's your entrance from the gardens."

Clive moved out from behind the yucca and tiptoed across the room.

"I can't look," said Roger.

"Shut up," said Derek and Clive in unison. "Now, Tessa," continued Derek, "you move around as if you can't see her; pretend to light a cigarette and settle yourself in one of these chairs. I'm going to come back in, see her, and drop my glass of whisky and soda."

"Are you going to break it?" asked Ethel.

"I'm going to pretend," said Derek. He strode purposefully to the kitchen hatch, picked up an imaginary glass, returned to the centre of the room, looked at Clive and said, "*My God!*"

"So camp," said Clive.

"Your turn, Tessa." Derek pointed at her line.

"*Charles.*" She wanted to cry.

"*Are you a ghost?*" said Derek to Clive.

"*I suppose I must be. It's all very confusing.*" Clive swished the bed sheet around his ankles.

"Up Pompeii," said Roger from a table in the corner. He turned over a jack of hearts.

"*Darling Charles – who are you talking to?*" said Tessa.

"She's missed a line," said Roger.

"All right, A. A. Gill," said Clive.

Derek deepened his voice. "*Elvira, of course. She's standing a few yards away from you.*"

"*Yes, dear,*" read Tessa, "*I can see her distinctly – under the piano with a zebra.*"

"*Oh God,*" Derek clutched his head, "*she's here, I tell you.*"

"*To hell with Elvira!*" shouted Tessa.

"That's my girl," said Derek. "Right on the money."

"*She's getting cross.*" Clive swished his bed sheet coquettishly.

Tessa threw the script across the room. "I'm not doing this any longer."

"Brilliant," said Clive.

"Yes, bravo," said Roger.

"*Shut up!*" said Derek.

"Fuck you all," said Tessa.

"I don't think that's in the script," said Roger.

14

TOTO

The cast were at the pub. Act Three in the bag, they'd piled down to the White Horse, all except Issy who'd got detention and missed rehearsals. Ros had got a lift in with Clare; she hadn't felt like driving and it meant she could drink. Peter had promised to pick Issy up and give both the girls supper. Clare, Brian, Diane and Barbara were cramped at a table; Diane sipped a white wine, Barbara nursed a whisky and coke, Brian slopped a pint and Clare stared into her Guinness. Scott and Ros were still at the bar.

"She says you came to see her. And she's pregnant."

"I hope the two aren't related," said Ros.

Scott laughed. "You didn't, did you?"

Ros found it hard to leave her character on the stage. Her poise half-turned as if the bar was the mantelpiece, she inspected her nails. When she spoke, her voice trailed vowels from the 1930s. "Poor Tess."

Scott dropped his chin to his pint, he was hunched on his elbows, arms crossed as if the bar was a pillow. "I didn't think so. You'd have to be fucking mad. She had this friend once, this do-good, you know the type? The ones who think they can sort everyone's life out? She was always going in

102

with audio tapes of gongs and shit, don't you hate people like that? Who think after five minutes of knowing your business, they can see it clear as day."

"What happened?"

"Tessa threw a brick at her; it was fucking funny, actually." He looked like he'd been run over by his own zebra Land Rover. His eyes were bloodshot, his hair stiff with sawdust, his nails crusted with dirt, the skin cracked; she had the urge to submerge him in a bath of olive oil. He'd fluffed his lines and Brian had patted him on the back and said, *Not to worry, old man.* Ros had the feeling Brian thought Tessa had left him. Thankfully, at least, he'd stopped asking.

Scott continued, "It always goes like this. First, she floods the house, then she blames the CIA, then she says I'm having an affair, and then she says she's pregnant."

"And are you?" She was only half-joking.

"Chance'd be a fine thing. Jesus. As if I haven't got enough on my plate."

"And she's definitely not pregnant – I mean, this time?"

Scott laughed again, but not in a way that made Ros feel loved. "You're a funny woman."

"No, I just meant—"

"Of course she's not fucking pregnant. Not unless it's an immaculate conception."

"I can imagine it getting pretty frisky in there." She thought of Derek and Clive and felt sick.

"That's because you've never been in there. It's no *Girl, Interrupted*, I can tell you. And it won't be me, either. We haven't had sex for months."

"Oh."

"Do you want another?" He slid her empty glass away

from her and leaned into the bar. "Tom, a lager, and another G and T. Double?"

"Why not," said Ros.

"And a packet of scratchings."

They took their drinks over to the others. Scott took the stool next to Clare; Ros hovered round the other side, where Brian and Barbara were already cramped. "Room for a small one?"

They shuffled along the bench. Brian shouted to the barman for another round, the barman rang the bell.

"Can't be," said Brian, trying to look at his watch.

"It's gone eleven," said Diane.

"My goodness!" said Barbara.

They all started to shift and move at once, Diane launching from her chair like a cloth cork from a bottle, Brian and Barbara shuffling along the bench away from Ros, who had to hurl her weight sideways to stop it tipping up like a seesaw. Diane passed everyone their coats.

Clare stood beside Ros, one arm in her Barbour. She held Ros's coat for her.

"I can take her back," said Scott.

"I see you two managed to get in a cheeky last one," said Brian.

"He was just closing up," said Scott.

"Don't keep him up all night." Diane helped Clare find her other sleeve.

"I'm not sure I should have had that second one." Barbara's heavy-knit cardigan rucked as she heaved herself into her beige mackintosh.

"Tomorrow and tomorrow and tomorrow," shouted Brian, his hand in the air as he was swept out on the wave of the pub emptying. Ros and Scott were left alone.

They talked of other things: Scott's business, Ros's garden, whether she should take down the oak or try to save it. They didn't stay long, the barman was wiping tables; soon, they were out in the biting night air, running across the empty car park to Scott's Land Rover.

"Should you be driving?" Ros climbed into the seat and gently clicked the door shut. She remembered hearing Scott shout at Tessa for slamming it. The catches were old. She wrapped her coat tighter around her, her black puffer jacket that was like wearing a duvet, a hood lined with fake fur, but still the freeze seeped in. She shivered. "Fuck, it's cold."

Scott got in the other side. There was something in the rangy sit of his limbs beside her that made her not want to look. She reached over her left shoulder for the seat belt.

"I wouldn't bother with that. I only pretend it's got belts for the MOT. They'd not save a fly."

She didn't know why Tessa complained so much about Scott's Land Rover. It was brilliant, solid, noisy and real. She felt like she was on safari. "Will we see elephants?" She clamped her hands between her knees to keep them warm.

"Only tigers at this time of night. And lions. We could camp up on the rise." He pointed at the black outline of the South Downs.

"*I hear the drums echoing tonight*, something-something *of some quiet conversation,*" sang Ros.

"*She's coming in, 12:30 flight,*" sang Scott, tapping beats on the steering wheel with his fingers and they both laughed.

Ros said, "12:30 flight?"

"Something like that, here." He got his phone out of his back pocket and passed it to her. "Find it."

It felt intimate, holding his phone as they bumped along, another window on his life. She scrolled through iTunes.

105

"It's on a playlist. Africa 4, I think. Toto."

"I know, it's, ah, got it." She pressed play and held it up between them. The opening chords, tinny on the phone speaker, made them sway in their seats. Ros clapped with exaggerated irony.

"*Hurry, boy, it's waiting there for you,*" sang Scott. He banged the drum roll out with the flat of his palms, his body moving, his chest, his shoulders, she couldn't look, she sang along, their voices wound together, and when they dropped into the quiet of the instrumental, Scott held up his finger in readiness, smiling sideways at her, not looking at the road. The cold had left her. She wanted to open a window and feel the freeze of night air.

He sang, "*The wild dogs cry out in the night.*"

"Ba-ba-baba, bababa, ba," sang Ros.

"*I know that I must do what's right.*" He threw another glance at her and laughed.

"Eyes on the road!" she squealed and together they sang, "*Serengeti,*" as if on duet at karaoke, their heads close, almost touching. She held his phone like a microphone between them.

An oncoming car lit the road. Scott dimmed his headlights. He looked so handsome in this darkness. The moon was out, almost full and misted by winter; an owl flew across their path.

"That's good luck, isn't it?" asked Ros.

"If you like," said Scott. He hummed the rest of the song. Ros rested his phone on her lap. They were nearly there.

"You know you were fabulous tonight." He kept his eyes forward.

"Oh, no, you were."

"I was shit, as you well know. Fuck knows how I'm going

to get it together. But you were great. I mean it. You've made everyone up their game."

"You're sweet. I do my best." If only they really could head for the hills and camp out under the stars. Fuck, she must be drunk. He pulled up outside her house.

"Bye, darling." She jumped down.

"Don't slam it." He leaned across the seat.

She closed it gently and waved. He waved back.

The house was quiet. She kicked off her shoes, put the kettle on, thought better of it and opened the fridge. A half-bottle of white wine, a nightcap. She poured herself a glass and got the pot from the bookshelves. Her laptop threw Apple light as she trawled through playlists till she found the one she wanted. She never thought she'd be able to listen to it again without pain.

Ben. It had been his fault, not hers. She put her feet up on the table, let the spliff take hold, chased it with a cooling sip of Sauvignon Blanc. Ben, and Cara's depression. Ben, and Cara's paranoia. Ben playing opposite her, his Colonel Vishinin to her Masha, a run at the Young Vic while Cara's run of post-partum psychosis went on just as long but without the applause.

Cara's baby had come out screaming and hadn't stopped; from baby to toddler to first day at nursery. Molly and Issy had never got half the attention Cara had slathered on Poppy and they'd done just fine. Black-out curtains, white noise apps, panic attacks at every stage from weaning to potty training to first day at school; Ros had said, *Just leave her, Car, crying never hurt anyone,* but the cracks in their friendship had begun to show. Attempts at playdates had ended in Molly throwing sand in Poppy's buggy and Cara deciding Poppy had an allergy to wheat. Primary school was one long asthma attack and complaints to the headmaster that Poppy wasn't getting enough *quiet time*. By the time Cara landed the role of Masha, Poppy was practically smoking behind the bike shed, and Cara's anxiety had reached a peak. Panic about lines, panic about costume fittings, Ros had said, *Oh god, who isn't self-harming these days? It's just a phase,* but apparently that was the last straw. Cara wouldn't let her babysit. What else was Ros supposed to do? Sit back and watch? Her contract on *Casualty* was almost up, she'd be dying in two episode's time. It was true that playing Masha was the perfect step from soap opera to stage, true that she already knew the part, that the production was a chance to be taken seriously. But she'd only popped into the theatre to see how it was getting on, it was only that she cared. Ben hadn't helped, swanning about looking like Alexander Skarsgård in a Cossack hat, persuading her to stand in when Cara cancelled again. Was it her fault they had chemistry? It wasn't as if she'd had to remind the director how much he'd loved her in audition. Ros refilled her glass and rolled another joint. It was lethal, the theatre, it had seduced them both. *Just get out of my life, Ros.* Those had been the last words her best friend had said to her. Well, she had.

But she'd forgotten the joy, the thrill, the buzz, the unutterable, intoxicating excitement. She closed her eyes and let fantasy take hold like the wine, the spliff, the songs that were playing, the feel of his arms, the touch of his hand, that voice. She could play a little, it did no one any harm, there was no one there to see inside her head. Why not have a little fun? Everything would return to normal when Tessa came home, of course it would, it was obvious he was just lonely.

15

LET ME OUT

But Tessa wasn't going anywhere. She'd kicked off in the lounge and Ethel had fainted for real. Her dressing gown stank, her hair was lank, her shins were thick with stubble. They'd called her into the office for a chat.

"How do you think it's going, Tessa?"

"I want to go home."

Two of the nurses raised their eyebrows; Dr Patel suppressed a smile.

"We'd like to try you on another medication."

Of course they would. That was their answer to everything. She wondered if they had a pill for unfaithfulness. Or betrayal.

"We're going to try you on a low dose of Prolixin."

It was because of the drugs that she'd lost the baby. She'd told them they weren't safe. No one ever believed her. Shuffle-shuffle down the corridor, stop in the entrance hall, the old-fashioned telephone on the wall, the noticeboard stuck with visiting times and pink leaflets suggesting meditation, the double airlock doors to the outside world. The lounge, the courtyard, her bedroom; where would she park herself for the next block of time? The chairs had been set up for group therapy at four. She shuffled to the courtyard. Time dragged.

One of these days, she'd get the hang of rolling cigarettes. She dropped half the tobacco on the paving. By the time she'd managed to light it, two drags put it out again and she chucked it at the wall. An ember fell on a late-winter daisy. She kicked it with her slipper. This was the worst of it; not the shouting and crying and the trauma and the fucking awful food, not the scratchy beds and nutters everywhere. It was the ache of time drawing to an almost close, it was the powerlessness to stop it. Tessa let the glass door slam behind her. At least the corridor was warm. She leaned against the wall, the nurse's station half an eye in view, their door open, she could hear them chatting, the occasional name she knew. Somewhere in that room or the one beyond where her psychiatrist sat in an upright chair, her kind eyes and organised hands, somewhere in there was a file with every Tessa word, and every Tessa action noted. There was no blood pressure chart or record of bowel movements, no physio report that she'd walked the corridor alone. They believed her illness was all in her mind where they could not go, and the record of her success and failure was measured like this, in behaviour, in phrases funnelled by their questions and filtered by their judgement. There was no trust, anywhere.

Shuffle-shuffle to group therapy. She retied the belt around her robe. Dr Patel had given up encouraging her to get dressed. What was the point? *It'll make you feel better.* But she'd be the judge of that, thank you very much, and her judgement, from many, many years of study, said it wouldn't. *It's a good habit to get into.* If they wanted to talk habits, how about the one where they gave her pills every time she acted up? If they couldn't throw their habits, they had no business with hers. *You don't want your visitors seeing you in your dressing gown, do you?* What visitors would they be? Her husband who didn't care? The woman he was fucking? She'd told him Ros had come to see her and he'd said, *I don't think so, love,* as if she'd make such a thing up. She'd have shown him the script if Ethel hadn't eaten it. Now, the only reason to get dressed was to get out. She'd managed to escape once; when Freddy was a baby, she'd run through the double doors to cheers from the lounge and got as far as her mother standing uselessly shouting while three nurses chased her around the car park. It had been fun. It was tradition. A habit.

The lounge filled up with the others. Tessa chose a seat facing the window in the absurd circle of straight-backed chairs on which they were expected to feel comfortable. Derek had already broken three. The one he was on now looked at the point of collapse.

"Are we all here?" The therapist with her legs crossed and her smile on. Tessa had thought about training as a therapist once, somewhere in a long run of being well, when she'd thought she'd conquered it, when Freddy had started nursery and she'd had time again on her hands.

"Depends what you mean by *here*," said a boy with floppy hair and black jeans.

Ethel looked panicked and Carrie giggled.

If only they were allowed to smoke, people might talk more. If they could sit around in armchairs as if they were at the pub, if there were an open fire and baskets of scampi and drinks on offer, she'd settle for a Coke, but if they could make it just a bit more *cheery* and stop treating them as though this was their fault, as if fat had caused it, or laziness, then maybe the inmates of Mercury Ward would start talking. If they could stop punishing them all the time.

"Who'd like to start?" The therapist wore a badge which said, *Sally Hopkins-Smythe*.

Everybody looked at the floor except Ethel, who looked at the ceiling.

If she said she was fine and played well, if she took her pills with gratitude and accepted her condition and the comprehension of the world that named her ill with no hope of a cure, if she played their game, swallowing their view as her own, Dr Patel would give her the kind of smile that said, *We're watching*. And if she kicked off, they upped her meds. She couldn't win. She was pinned, labelled, as much at war with her past as they were with her future. Did she have to accept their diagnosis if they were to let her out? Yes. Did she believe to her core that they were wrong? Double yes. But it felt as if the professional members of the section ward were a team united against her – a secret enclave of discussion. She needed her voice heard, the connections she'd made, made valid in the eyes of authority. Why wouldn't they listen? *Think of it like diabetes... You'd take insulin, wouldn't you?... Your brain's misfiring, that's all* – a chemical imbalance that had nothing to do with her childhood, a fact like diabetes that couldn't be helped. Yet these fallen that she sat among had traumas in common. They shared stories of abandonment and neglect. Not one of them had arrived by accident; all of them were scarred.

"Carrie?"

Carrie wound a thread around her finger, turning the tip blue.

"Would you like to say anything?" Sally Hopkins-Smythe wore jeans from the eighties and ballet pumps. If Tessa worked for MIND, she'd wear a flak suit.

Carrie shook her head. She wound the thread the other way.

"Roger?"

Roger had found his way to cope. "I'd appreciate it if Miss Noggins over there—"

"Do you mean Ethel?"

"Ethel the unready," said Clive.

"I do ask that you abide by the code, Roger, all of you, of patience, love and listening, while you're in this room. Ethel has a name."

Ethel crossed her arms and bared her teeth, an animal in belted shawl, rope around her waist, grey socks.

"I'd appreciate it if everyone left my cards alone," said Roger.

"Roger that," said Derek. Clive laughed.

"I'm sure we can do that," said Sally. "Can't we, Ethel? Respect each other's space? We're all here to get better."

"Is that what you're here for?" asked Clive.

"Tessa," Sally Hopkins-Smythe turned tired eyes upon her. "Maybe you'd like to start us off."

If she'd been held, if she'd felt for an instant that she was safe, if, after she'd been shut in the cupboard and told she was going to die, the Alice in Wonderland drugs, her sisters laughing, if after all of that her mother had held her and said, *My darling, how awful, it will never happen again*; if her mother had protected her from the myriad times it had happened before and would happen again instead of saying in that bright kitchen, not stopping for a minute with the carrots she was chopping, not even turning around but saying with her back, her hair, sleeves up, *Do stop making things up, Theresa. Go and wash your hands. Your sisters were having a joke. They only tease you because they love you*; if none of that had happened, who knew where she'd be now? Not in Mercury Ward, slumped in an uncomfortable chair beside a dying yucca plant, surrounded by loss.

"I want to go home."

"Do you feel ready to go home?"

"Yes."

"Do you want to talk a little about coping mechanisms?"

"She doesn't think she's ill," blurted Carrie.

"Shall we let Tessa speak?" Sally Hopkins-Smythe had a wedding ring on, and gold studs, and a thin gold chain around her neck.

"Exercise, nutrition, sleep," said Tessa. It reminded her of the midwife who'd come in to help after Freddy was born – *to show her the ropes,* as if it was as simple as that. *We call it the E-A-S-Y method; eat-activity-sleep-you.* The acronym had made Tessa feel lonely. They should have called it H-A-R-D. Hopelessness-anger-regret-despair. It had felt like that; everyone watching, waiting for her to fuck it up, hovering constantly to whip him away from her. It was all very well to tell her about the E-A-S-Y method, but what about telling Freddy? All he'd wanted was her and all she'd wanted was him. Wasn't that what mothers were supposed to feel? She'd read that for the first three months, babies weren't even aware they were separate.

"Exactly right," said Sally. "A routine of exercise, a balanced diet and regular sleep."

"And medication," said Ethel.

"Thank you, Ethel. And, of course, taking your medication. Do you think you can manage that, Tessa?"

If she said yes, would they let her out? "Yes."

Freddy had been four months old when they'd taken her away in an ambulance and locked her up here, her first time in Mercury Ward, ten years ago. Wasn't that post-natal depression? Other women suffered it, but they didn't get locked up. Or maybe they did. That was the fear, wasn't it? If you tell anyone that you're on the edge, that you're out of your mind with exhaustion, they'll take your baby away from you, so you don't. You don't say anything until it's too late. What was it about this habit they loved so much of ripping the fragile away from the only binds keeping them anchored to the ground? The vulnerable needed connection, not isolation. Motherhood was frightening enough, but without Freddy it was impossible.

"And do you want to talk a little about your worries around going home?" She had brown bobbed hair that trembled every time she spoke. The chain around her neck had a thin gold cross on it.

Tessa searched her mind for the right thing to say. Everyone got it wrong sometimes, didn't they? Everyone ignored advice and stumbled through, finding their own way. A friend from NCT had hidden in her bathroom, scared of what she might do to her baby who hadn't stopped crying for fourteen hours. Had they locked her up? No. They'd said she was suffering exhaustion and brought in help. Or Clare, who'd nearly blinded Nancy with Olbas Oil when she'd poured too much on the pillow in the middle of the night while animal shapes danced in shadows on the wall. Or the time Ros had told them about when she'd topped up a carton of apple juice with vodka and forgotten and given it to Molly and Issy for three breakfasts in a row.

"Tessa?" said Sally.

Had anyone called them incompetent? Had anyone said they were a danger? No. They'd laughed about it. No one had laughed when Freddy had rolled off the bed. No one had said, *This whole thing's a nightmare; you're doing great,* when she ran into her mother in Sainsbury's and had it reported over dinner that night that she'd been seen rocking the peas to sleep. They didn't laugh and say, *Been there, done that*; they exchanged looks. They gave that flags-up straightening of the mouth.

"I just think I'm ready."

Sally nodded, her hair trembled, and Carrie wound the thread the other way.

Tessa shifted position on the uncomfortable, hard-backed, hard-seat chair. They'd said she wasn't safe, but without Freddy in her arms, there'd been no point at all. They'd removed him and expected her to calm down. She'd learnt more about playing the game that time than she ever had before. Shut up and pretend. That was the message. Nobody was interested in the horror of a child out of reach, nobody took any notice. They called it another episode.

"That is good to hear," said Sally. "It's good to hear you're making progress."

She was in for four months that time. When she came out, she found it hard to touch him. H-A-R-D. He'd been weaned, of course. They'd had to feed him. Changing his nappy for the first time after, a health visitor had watched over her shoulder while pretending to fold muslins. He wasn't hers anymore. Everybody had said it hadn't affected him at all.

Tessa ground to a halt in the corridor. The floor was a dirty-pink linoleum; the walls, magnolia and scuffed. She wasn't sure how she'd got there or when group therapy had finished. She'd just drifted to a stop. Her hair was lanky and her dressing gown was loose. Where was she going? Why was she here? None of it made any sense.

16

LYING TO SCOTT

Ros convinced herself she wasn't an alcoholic on a daily basis. Of course she wasn't. She just liked a glass. Half the time it was medicinal and, anyway, it was better to be consistent than boom and bust. Obviously she'd have a clean out in the spring, a *Dry January* or a ten-day juice fast; she used to beg Harold for a stay at the Mayr Clinic, apparently you could bump into Tracy Emin at the herbal tea bar, but he'd told her she could just as easily not drink at home for free. Fucking Harold. He hadn't had to put up with yoga mums eyeing each other's thighs in Daylesford Café while going on about sugar and how much they adored wheatgrass. It was no wonder she drank. They all did. Anyway, white wine wasn't fattening. Everyone knew that. And she could stop any time. She finished off the bottle of Pinot and opened another. The house was quiet, the dogs asleep, the girls were out. All she wanted was an hour to herself and she'd be fine. It wasn't her fault her nerves were on edge. The whole thing was getting to her. She adjusted her chair on the uneven floor. The wine tasted delicious. So did her Marlboro. She exhaled and felt reasonable thoughts flood through her.

She should never have got involved in the first place. She knew there was a reason she'd given it up. She was too highly strung. Too sensitive. She simply didn't know how to not give it her all. Amateurs tossed lines about like sticks, put on voices and took them off again, pretended, but she *became*; there was a difference, she couldn't help it. She wasn't a professional for nothing.

She'd always been like that, even as a child doing shows in the front room, she'd taken it seriously, immersed herself completely, hadn't understood how her parents could get bored, leave halfway through, or not turn up at all. Peter had sat through some of them, jollied on by their mother, but he'd got distracted, too, started playing with his Action Man; it had generally ended in tears. Soft toys and dolls had filled the gap until she'd discovered the actual stage, a real stage at primary school where she wasn't a sheep or third angel for long, where, aged nine, she was cast as Mary. She could have lived in that moment forever, the blue dress, the headscarf with white trim, the plastic Jesus in her arms that doubled as everyone's baby when the girls played washing-up. She used to fight over it, too, until the nativity changed her world; after that, only the wedding gown and veil from the dressing-up box would do; who wanted a baby anyway when there was an audience to please – she didn't have time. She would spend her lunch break trailing torn white lace and refuse to go outside unless the wind was blowing in the right direction; how could she exit the building if the train weren't lifted in a river behind her? What good was a dramatic pause if there was no one there to see it? That no one took enough notice, mattered only as long as it took to build an audience in her mind; in her imaginary world, contained within the brick and cement playground, the parquet floors and crowded classrooms, she decided a sell-out show, a deafening applause, an audience of thousands who never took their eyes off her at all. Walking home with Peter after school was *cameras, lights, action!;* a director devoted, telling her how beautifully she'd done that scene, telling her she was perfect; a tilt of the head here, a sideways smile there, the subtlest glimmer in the eye. She was a star in her own school uniform, an Oscar winner as she ate her tea, an actress adored who felt a little lonely inside when she went to bed, but that, as she told her teddy, was the price of fame.

She topped up her glass. Funny how these memories came back. She'd known from the outset that she would be an actress. It was in her blood. No matter what she did, it would never let her go. Doing the play had reawakened something, a yearning, a desire only satisfied with bright lights and, even then, only for those moments. The want rushed in as quickly as the curtain dropped; why had she left it so long? She lit another cigarette. She knew why. It was too big, too great, too deep. She'd shut it out, hoping that would shut it up. But it had only waited, silent, full of power. It would never leave her.

That was how she saw it, anyway. She wasn't aware that a drip feed of neglect, a daily laceration of the missing can lead a faith to break, an omnipotence to be born, a mind to opt for fantasy and a body to be so riddled with discomfort that to live among its screaming nerve endings becomes a thing impossible. So subtle had been the lack, so consistent, so hidden by the appearance of plenty, that when she looked back on her childhood, the absence of her parents' care read as normal. Instead of seeing the pattern on repeat, she lived as if the yawning gap within her was for want of something given her today.

Another week of rehearsals, another Friday night doing Freddy's tea and the cool sense of control she'd had when had Scott dropped her off after the pub had been replaced by the dawning of another, more disturbing, sensation. It couldn't be. She must be imagining it.

Last Friday, he'd rung to ask if she could possibly pick Freddy up from school; a complicated arrangement with Barbara taking over at nine meant that she hadn't seen him. He'd left the key under the mat for her and a note on the table saying, *You're an angel. I owe you*, and for a split second she'd thought it said, *I love you*. Had he done that on purpose? It was too impossible to contemplate. She kept it anyway. She folded it up and put it in her purse.

The weekend had passed quietly. Molly and Issy had been at their dad's; he'd picked them up on Saturday morning. She hated him intruding on her life here, turning up in his stupid sports car. He could at least get a Porsche and not some knock-off from Japan. She'd stayed upstairs, watching from the window, waiting for the door to slam and hadn't come down until he'd driven away, Molly in the front, Issy squished in the back.

She'd planned on going to the spa. The brochure was still open on her laptop – a massage, a sauna, a swim – but it was too cold to go out, and on Sunday it rained, so she'd stayed in bed and watched *Outlander*. On Tuesday, Scott had shown up at rehearsals looking battered. She'd kept her distance. They'd walked through scenes like automatons. Everyone was getting tense; maybe it was that. Or maybe he was fighting it as hard as she was. On Thursday, he'd had to leave early, she hadn't bothered going to the pub with the others, the play felt like it was falling apart, and today was Friday, another Friday, her life had become marked by them.

She looked at her phone. She'd texted him asking how he was doing, but had heard nothing back. Just as she determined to forget the whole thing, have a bath, congratulate herself on not falling down that rabbit hole, it pinged its little notice, making her jump. She glanced, trying to be casual even though there was no one watching.

knackered

She could have sent a sad face emoji and shut that shit down. But Molly was at Nancy's and Issy was on a school sleepover, and Ros was bored. She picked an upside-down smiley face and pressed send.

His answer came back a few minutes later. Enough time for her to roll through doubt, regret, flippancy and fuck you.

want to come over?

She had to get a grip. This was what theatre did to you. Chemistry was the danger that worked. You had to feed it, but keep it on a leash – that was what she'd learnt. Feed it, but keep it on a leash, because when the curtain came down on the last show of the run, that would be that; the spell would be broken and they'd all go back to their lives. You had to believe you were in love, it was all part of the play. Scott knew that. They were both playing. She was sure of it.

As she downed her glass, no point in wasting it, picked up her bag, shrugged on her coat, shut the dogs in the utility and turned off the lights, she had no intention of saying anything about Harold. She was thinking how glad she was she'd made a casserole that morning, so she didn't have to rush into Midhurst and turn up with another lasagne from Cook. She sat the Le Creuset on the passenger seat beside her and put the belt around it so that it didn't slide off.

He opened the door in his tracksuit, a Fair Isle cardigan slung over the top of a Ramones T-shirt she recognised from doing the ironing last week. While he helped Freddy with his homework, she reorganised the kitchen drawers. He'd said a few times that the cutlery was in the wrong place. It should be on the other side, in the drawers below the cupboard with the missing door and the crack snaking up the side. She'd always thought Tessa was exaggerating about her kitchen needing doing.

Waiting for the potatoes, she moved quietly about the utility room, taking clothes out of the drier and folding them up. The laundry basket was full of Scott's work clothes and Freddy's sports kit. She put on another wash.

Scott set the table. Freddy went off upstairs and returned in his pyjamas.

"I hope you like venison." She poured them each a glass of red and refilled Freddy's cup with water. They ate in silence for a while, the atmosphere too perfect to break. Ros picked at her food. It was hard to feel hungry and happy at the same time. Glistening gravy, smooth and buttery mash, Scott went to the pantry and came back with mustard. These details she was learning. She'd remember for next time.

"She's a fine cook, isn't she, Fred?"

Freddy nodded.

Ros smiled. "Well, thank you. It's a pleasure. My girls don't seem to bother with food."

"You're wasted on them."

"They get it from their father. He's like a piece of wire. Salad, that's what he liked. And fish."

"I hate fish," said Freddy.

"Then I shall make a note not to cook it."

"You'd have a career as a private chef, no trouble," said Scott, piling mash onto his fork.

"You're sweet. It's not difficult."

"Difficult for some. And that was you, was it? Or our Babs?"

"That was me, what?" She ate a carrot.

"Who cleaned out the pantry."

She laughed. "Have you only just noticed?"

"Christ, Freddy, who let her go?" Scott scuffed his son's hair. "You come across a woman like Ros, you grab her with both hands, do you hear? You don't let her go."

"Oh shucks, you two. It's nothing. I'm a tidier. I can't help it." She felt warm inside. She felt warm everywhere.

Scott put his knife and fork together.

Ros said, "Will you have more?"

"I'm done. Come on Fred-Fred. Eat up. You can watch a bit of telly."

Ros cleared the plates while Scott tucked Freddy up on a beanbag with the biscuit tin. She put the dishwasher on. He came back with a bottle of whisky. They both got their tobacco out. The sound of *Power Rangers* filtered in from the snug.

"Just a small one," said Ros as Scott unscrewed the lid.

"A finger." He gave her that devilish smile that made everything dirty. Ros looked away.

"Fuck." He rubbed his face. "What a week. Sorry about last Friday. I was stuck in Alton with a client who kept changing his mind. There's not a lot you can do if you've already cut the fucking tree down."

The whisky was hot and dry in her throat. It made her head swim. "I was dealing with my ex all week. I wish I could cut him down."

"Difficult, is he?"

Ros shook her head; her hair fell tousled across her face. "You don't know the half of it."

"I don't know the any of it. How long were you married?"

"Thirteen years, but the divorce took another two."

She remembered his face when she'd said, *I'm not leaving. I've nowhere to go*, and he'd said, *You've done this to yourself, Ros. It's over. You're going to have to deal with it.*

"Was it you who left him?"

It was her who'd done the actual leaving. "We just came to the end of the road."

"A woman like you. You'll not be single for long, not round here. They'll be queuing up."

"I think I'm done for a while. All the good ones are taken."

Scott put his feet up and waggled his toes. "You never know."

"I still feel bruised." She sipped her whisky. "And I worry Issy's going to be like him. Sorry. Maybe I shouldn't talk about it. I mean, with Fred."

"Fred's not here."

"No, I mean, with Tessa having her illness, and Freddy."

"It's not catching." He leaned towards her, turning his glass on the table, "Was that what it was? Your ex? Was he not right in the head?"

Her father used to say that assumption was the mother of all fuck-ups, but Scott's face had whisky-softened and there was a light in his eyes as if a door had opened on another room. She bit her nail.

"Christ, Ros." He leaned back and put his feet up again on Freddy's chair. "All this time with me bleating on. You should have said." Those crinkly green eyes looking right at her. "You know, I only call the police when she's a danger to Fred. I can deal with no end of shit. I don't care if she burns the fucking house down, but Fred…" He ran his hand through his hair. A stray pine needle fell to his shoulder; Ros had the urge to wipe it away. "People don't understand. They think she should pull herself together and I'm such a martyr for putting up with it. It's so fucking hard to explain."

She said, "I tried."

"It doesn't matter how hard you try."

"I had to get the girls away."

"It's the most selfish illness there is."

"It's probably not the same."

"Sure."

"I mean you and Tess love each other."

"Sure, we do."

"I'm sure you'll be fine."

"We'll see."

She'd finished her whisky. "I better get going."

Scott had been staring into space. He got up. "You all right to drive?"

What was the alternative? She didn't want to think about it. "I'll be fine. How's she getting on?"

"Same."

"Any news on when she'll be out?"

He shook his head. She put on her coat, he held the door, she moved past him quickly, rushing for the cold night air as the cold night air rushed in. If she'd stopped, she was sure he would have kissed her.

17

LYING TO CLARE

She needed her head examined. That's what she needed. She needed a frontal lobotomy. Last night they'd kissed. He'd put his arms around her and kissed her. It was the following day. She'd had a lie-in. It was gone eleven. She spat toothpaste into the bathroom sink and wiped her mouth. Maybe if she told someone. Maybe if she heard it out loud it would vanish.

She couldn't tell her analyst. He wouldn't understand. She examined her face in the mirror. There was no way she could confide in Peter and Diane. She'd already made that mistake; she'd told them she'd been doing Freddy's tea. Peter had said, *You want to watch that. Man on his own. Wife in a state*, and Diane had chipped in, *You certainly have chemistry on stage.* She'd replied, *God, you two. Will you credit me with a little maturity? I'm not fourteen*, and Peter had said, *If you were fourteen, I'd tell Scott to stand well back.* She pulled her cheeks gently away from her mouth with the tips of her fingers. Fucking jowls. One of God's cruel jokes. The more you laughed, the worse they got. She could almost pass for fourteen, or maybe twenty-five, if she had a nip and tuck. But what was it Joan Rivers said? You could choose old or weird. Young was only available to the young. She applied another layer of Neal's Yard Rejuvenating Serum to her eyes, ruffled her hair loose from its scrunchy, went down to the kitchen, let the dogs out and, while the kettle boiled for coffee, she rang Clare.

*

They met in Cowdray Café. Clare, already at a table by the window, waved and half got up when she saw her, then changed her mind. Ros shrugged off her coat. They both looked at the board.

Clare said, "What are you having?" She was her usual harried meets straw, cheeks rosy, hers weren't sagging, maybe it was all that fresh air.

"I don't know." Ros unwound her scarf. "Maybe the soup."

The café was an add-on to the shop, a revitalisation of old buildings that had once stored grain and tractors, now done up to make Londoners feel safe. Enough dirt, but not too much, chalkboards telling of provenance and nurture, it served what the shop sold – wonky heritage carrots and Brian's grass-reared steak, pockmarked fruit, and local cheese, each turned into glazed this and thinly sliced that, wooden platters with hunks of Sussex brie, bowls of thick green soup that cost as much as a burger on the high street.

Clare went to order while Ros stared out the window. Mud and leaves, weak winter sun, a car park of Range Rovers and personalised number plates spelling K8TEE and B3RT. Harold had promised to get her one. He never had. A few spattered pickups. Clare's Subaru. A Land Rover like Scott's except not zebra-striped; she found she was looking for it everywhere. A child refused to put on its boots by an open hatchback, a mother struggled, a dog, trailing its lead, ran loose.

Clare came back with two large, thick-rimmed cups spilling cappuccino froth onto saucers. "To keep us going." She lowered them carefully to the table.

Ros mopped hers up with a napkin. "How's Nance?"

"Recovering." Blonde hair in her eyes, Clare swiped it away with the back of her hand leaving a smudge of mud on her forehead. "Did Molly tell you?"

"You told me." Ros passed her another napkin and pointed at her own forehead, almost doing the spit and wipe as if Clare was a child. Sometimes she felt like a child to Ros, liking everyone, everyone liking her, sailing along free of worries; she had them, of course she did, her daughter who she talked about, her love life which she didn't, but none of it seemed to rock her. She was like a tiny boat with an enormous tiller, steering a course no matter how rough the seas, skimming the waves no matter how big. It was irritating. Ros wished she could scupper her, just for a minute, just to see what lay beneath.

"Not about the break-up. The Facebook stuff." Clare scuffed the napkin over her forehead sending mud dust crumbling into the froth of her coffee. She absently stirred it in.

Ros felt slightly revolted. "Molly doesn't tell me anything."

"He was trolling her or something, whatever it's called. She blocked him. I had to tell school."

"Poor Nance."

"It's a fuck of an age to be a teenager, all this tech, cyber, social fuckery. It's everywhere. They can't escape it."

"Being a teenager is a nightmare full stop. We suffered the same." Ros ripped a tube of sugar.

"We didn't have our suffering plastered all over the internet, though, did we? We weren't cutting ourselves."

"Is Nancy cutting herself?"

"No, but there are girls she knows."

Ros sat back. "I was sniffing glue at the back of the science lab."

"I was going to clubs," said Clare, smiling. "How's Moll? Have you spoken to Fuck Face?"

"I emailed him."

"Do you think he'll kick up a fuss?"

"I don't care if he kicks up a fuss. They're not going skiing with him. Moll will be right in the middle of her mocks."

"They're not till May."

"She'll be revising for them."

"I can't understand how he's even allowed to see them."

Ros tried to remember what she'd told her. Had she been specific? She'd been so hungover and it was ages ago, she couldn't really remember. All she knew was that she'd had a feeling Clare's ex used to beat her up. Why else wouldn't she talk about him? Why such secrecy? She'd said as much to Tessa once. Tessa had said, *Isn't that a bit racist?* She was only joining the dots.

Ros waved it away, as if she, too, didn't want to talk about it. She didn't, anyway. She wanted to talk about Scott.

Their soups arrived, slopping and frothing in the same green porcelain. Two thick-cut pieces of seeded granary bread on a plate between them, a slab of butter in a little white dish. Clare took a slice, tore off a piece, buttered and dipped it. The café was loud with the clattering of dropped cutlery, tills ringing and children running, crammed with mothers wiping snot. Mostly women. *Nearly all women*, thought Ros, looking around. Young ones with toddlers, not quite middle-aged ones like her and Clare, a few roaring fifties deep in the menopause, and heaps of olds, crunched at pine tables getting carrot ribbons caught in their teeth. They should have had the soup, too. Ros picked up her spoon. Pea and mint. She chewed a strand of parsley.

Clare dipped another piece of bread. "Nance has never been skiing."

"We should take them sometime. Peter has a chalet."

"I've never been either."

"It'd be fun. We could get a bunch of us together."

"Not Brian."

"No, of course not. Christ. Unless you want him to come?"

"Very funny." Clare slurped at her spoon. "Have you seen Scott?"

"Yes, definitely Scott."

"No, sorry, I meant, have you *seen* him? He looks fucked."

Ros had been dreaming of the slopes. And her soup had too much salt in it. She felt hot. "I expect he's just tired. He said she never asks about Freddy."

"When did he say that?"

"Oh, the other day. I was over there for dinner. I took Freddy's tea round."

"That was nice of you."

"I've been doing it every Friday, actually."

"Aren't you the Samaritan."

"It's the least I can do."

"After what?"

"After nothing. I mean, I feel sorry for him, that's all, and I took Tessa's part, so it can't be easy."

"It's just a play, Ros. Tessa's really ill. I should get round there."

"I'm happy doing it."

"Has he been charming you? He'll be wanting you to do his socks next."

"I have been doing his socks."

Clare buttered another piece of bread.

The first time, or the first time they nearly had, it was she who'd turned her face away and they'd both looked sheepish and laughed and he'd made some joke about getting her next time. Next time he had. Next time she hadn't turned her cheek to him, she'd looked him dead in the eye as he'd grabbed her. Their lips had met and the room had gone completely quiet, at least that's how it had felt to her, her head so silent, her body caught in the absolute break point of the moment. Afterwards, Brian had clapped and said, *Bravo*, and the rest of the cast, watching from the wings, had started talking as if there was a rush-on. Clare had seen it, too – she must have.

Ros stirred the remains of her coffee. "What I mean is, I think he's handling it really well. Tessa's really lucky to have him."

"He's no angel."

"I never said he was."

"I'm just saying, he's not perfect."

"I know he's not perfect."

Clare had nearly finished her soup and eaten most of the bread. She wiped a crust around the bowl. Ros pushed her own bowl away, folded her arms on the table and leaned forward. "I'm just saying you should have seen the state of the place when I got there. I know Tessa's no Martha Stewart, but, still, there are limits."

Clare was trying to put her coat on while still sitting down.

Ros said, "I'm only trying to help."

"I'd better get going." Clare stood up, taking the chair with her. There was a clattering as she disentangled her Barbour from stained yellow pine.

Ros stayed seated. "I don't understand what I've done."

Clare said, "It's easy for people to think he's so great and she's so ill, you know? But he's just a guy like any other."

"What would you know about any other guys?"

Straw escaped her pockets as she searched for her car keys. She didn't look up as she set off for the door, weaving between tables. Ros found herself scrambling after her. Cold air hit her with a swipe.

"I didn't mean it, Clare. Stop. I didn't mean you don't know him better. Or Tess. Of course you know them better. It's just, going round there, I've got to know him."

Through the shop car park of stone walls, a fountain, wooden wheelbarrows of turnips and swedes and out into mud and Range Rovers parked in rows. Ros tied her scarf about her neck. "I can handle Scott."

Clare opened her door to the wagging tail of her terrier.

"Fucking hell, Clare – I wish I'd never mentioned it. I'm just helping out."

Clare stopped with one hand on her dog's collar. The wind blew her hair across her eyes. She wiped her nose with the back of her hand. "It may not look like it, Ros, but Tess and Scott are solid. They've had years of it. He might say he's sick of it, and God knows he is, they both are, but it's an illness, it's not her. She doesn't do it on purpose. I mean, sure, there are things she could do to help herself; she could stay on her meds, she could tidy the fucking kitchen and stop going on about changing it—"

"Actually, it really could do a with a bit of a—"

"It's not the fucking kitchen that's the problem, Ros. I've had years of it and they're both as bad as each other; they both blame the outside when it's the inside that's the problem. They both have demons; they both drink too much. Why do you think he left Derry? Tessa isn't the only one running. And Scott loves her. He might bitch from here till Sunday, but he married her. He knew what he was buying into, at least as much as anyone can know. You know she had her first episode on honeymoon? She threw their wedding rings in the Orinoco River. It's not funny, Ros, it's tragic. Fine, do his fucking tea, but don't buy into the 'poor Scott' routine, okay?"

"I wasn't asking your permission."

Clare got into her car and shut the door. Ros tapped on the window. Clare started the engine.

"Clare." The Subaru was ancient. It took an age for the window to squeak open. "Clare, I didn't mean it. I know you're worried."

"It's fine." It didn't look fine.

Ros tried to hug her, arm snaked through the window, elbow against the steering wheel.

When she released her, Clare said, "He loves her, Ros. He's always loved her."

"Of course he does," Ros replied, giving her best conciliatory smile, but when she got into her own car, she saw his eyes, his lips, the lazy range of his Irish limbs and thought, *You're wrong.*

18   POPPY

*"I love you." He put his arms around her, he pulled her
close and they kissed; a long, lingering explosion that made
her knees weak and her stomach flip. She put her hand on his
chest and pushed him away. "We have to tell—"*

"Mum?"

Ros saw Issy at the window. "What?" She exhaled a
plume of smoke into the air. Sometimes a cigarette was the
perfect cigarette. Sometimes the timing was just right.

"I can't find my charger."

That was all she got from her youngest these days;
perfunctory statements based on need.

"Look in Moll's room."

"She's locked it." Issy stood shivering at the back door.

"Use mine. It's…" she waved vaguely towards the house,
"somewhere. Try my desk."

"It's for an i8."

"Oh for Christ's sake, Iss, I don't know." She stubbed
her cigarette out on the leg of the table. Thanks, Harold, for
getting them new phones without asking her.

Issy had already disappeared into the house. Ros stretched
her arms over her head and yawned. She hadn't got anywhere

today. The morning had passed posting notices of the show on Facebook with exclamation marks and gifs of Scarlett O'Hara tearing down curtains. She'd thought about supper while eating a three-bean salad straight out of the plastic carton at the kitchen table, feet up, scrolling through Twitter, and got a ready meal out of the freezer to defrost before collecting the girls off the bus from school. Already dark, the sky was dotted with stars twinkling between the bare branches of the plane tree that towered at the end of her garden. It reminded her of London. She'd better get on with food. The fish pie wouldn't cook itself. She felt her phone buzz in her pocket. Probably Issy calling from her room. Or Scott. Maybe Scott. But it wasn't Issy or Scott. It was *Cara Deacon – missed call.*

She went into the kitchen, dropped her phone on the worktop and stared at it. *Cara Deacon – missed call.* Cara? Why was she calling? It had been, Ros counted on her fingers, nearly three years. Poppy would be almost thirteen. Every year her birthday popped up on Ros's phone, and every year she thought about sending a card. She'd even considered doing it anonymously, a little present in the post, no note. She didn't see why Poppy had to lose a godmother just because her own mother was a fucking psycho. Molly had, of course. But Molly didn't mind. She'd never been that interested in Cara. But Ros had always prided herself on being close to Poppy, even fancied that Poppy preferred her. They used to have such fun going off for babyccinos at the café in the park while Cara had another panic attack in a darkened room. She used to bring her back with chocolate down her front and sticky fingers and Cara would whisk her away as if she was infected.

She peeled off the cellophane lid, fitted the fish pie into the ceramic dish that made it look home-made and slid it into the Aga. Maybe she missed her. Maybe, after all this time, she was sorry.

She sat on the table, her feet on a chair, her elbows resting on her knees. They'd both withdrawn in the aftermath, wounds still bleeding; they hadn't spoken once. Her analyst had said she'd shown immense self-control in walking away. She'd let it go, superficially anyway. She'd taken a deep breath and thought, *Fine, have it your way. We'll see who the bigger person is. I know the truth. That's all that matters.* She'd walked away and Cara, Ben and Poppy had disappeared. She'd thought she'd never see them again. But if there was one thing she wasn't, it was a coward. She uncorked a half-bottle of Pinot, poured a generous glass, lit a cigarette and leaned into the phone as it rang.

The voice, when it picked up, didn't sound like Cara's.

"Car? It's Ros."

"Roselyn? This is Anne."

Cara's mother had always said Ros was a bad influence.

"Caroline asked me to call you."

"She rang me."

"I rang you."

"Oh, right, I see, but she—"

A scuffle of muffled voices, then Cara. "Ros?"

She'd always felt like an older sister to Cara; she'd known when there was something wrong sometimes even before Cara did. Cara could never hide anything from her.

"Car? What is it? What's going on?"

As if they'd never parted, as if they'd spoken yesterday. If something had happened, if Cara needed her, she'd drop everything, of course she would. She'd be there.

"Ros. Poppy." A muffle again, the faint voice of Cara. "I can't say it." A silence, a space, two people breathing, a

136

phone being handed over. Anne's voice came back on the line. "We've lost Poppy, Roselyn. Caroline wanted you to know."

What is this thing called shock? It's white noise, it's the brain working quickly, it's unreasonable behaviour and self-preservation, it's logic.

She must have sat for ages, the phone dead in her hands, her feet on the chair, her elbows resting on her knees. The moment when they'd found her. The moment the police came. The moment when they'd taken her away. The hours after, of already having to live with it, the alabaster skin of Poppy in the morgue. *They asked us if there was anyone who could come over, a neighbour, a friend, to sit with us.* She'd wanted to say, *I don't know how you keep breathing,* but she couldn't because Poppy hadn't. She'd stopped of her own accord.

Ros walked across the lane to her brother's house, the night black, the air crisp. Peter and Cara had always got on well. There was a time when their mothers had been sure they'd marry, but Cara had met Ben, and Peter had married Diane, and that had been that. She let herself in. The kitchen was warm. Peter leaned against the island. The moment she saw him she knew he knew. He put his arms around her. The tenderness felt uncommon. She held her face in her hands.

Peter rested his chin on her head. "Where are the girls?"

"Home." Ros released herself from her brother. She needed another drink.

"I'll make supper. Give them a call." Peter walked over to the fridge, opened it, stared at it.

He made bolognese. Ros watched him from the window seat. Diane came in. She put down shopping bags and sailed immediately to Ros to hug her. Ros's face was wet, her eyes puffy, her hands shook. The ashtray on the floor beside her was full. She knocked over her wine glass while reaching for it. "Shit."

"Never mind." Diane picked it up and got a cloth.

"Sorry."

"I'll get you another."

Molly and Issy wandered in.

"Are there mushrooms in it?" Issy leaned over the stove, looking at the bubbling pot.

"Issy," said Ros.

"I'm just asking. What's the matter with her?"

Peter looped his arm across his niece's shoulders. "You can pick them out."

"You two set the table," said Diane. "We'll eat in here."

Peter drained the linguine, Molly grated the Parmesan, Diane opened a bottle of red. Ros stared out of the window.

"You should eat something, too," said Peter.

"What's happened?" asked Molly.

"You girls sit down," said Diane, wiping her hands on a tea towel. She poured Issy and Molly glasses of water.

"Can I have a wine?" said Molly.

"No." Ros got up.

"Clare lets Nancy have beer."

"Well, I'm not Clare," snapped Ros, bursting into tears again, or maybe she hadn't stopped, maybe she'd never stopped crying since Cara said, *Get out of my life.*

Peter served and they all picked up their forks, passed the Parmesan, twirled pasta. All except Ros, who stared at her plate.

Peter put his fork down and wiped his mouth. "Your mother's had a shock, girls. Well, we all have, actually." He glanced quickly at Diane, and Diane stretched her hand out to Ros. Ros buried her face in her napkin, pushed her chair away, got up, taking her wine with her.

"What's happened?" asked Issy.

Peter said, "Do you remember Cara?"

"Peter," said Ros from the window seat.

"My godmother, Cara?" said Molly.

"That's right," said Peter.

"And Poppy?" said Issy. "Dad knows them." She twirled linguine on her fork.

"Issy," said Molly.

"What?" said Issy, her mouth full.

"Harold?" said Ros.

"Everybody calm down," said Peter.

But Ros was already on her feet. She put her hand on the back of Issy's chair. "Does Dad see them?"

"Uh-huh." Issy nodded. "Ow."

"When does he see them?"

"Molly hit me!"

"I didn't hit you."

"Why don't you sit down?" said Diane to Ros.

"When does he see them?"

"I don't think it matters, does it?" said Peter.

"Doesn't matter? Doesn't matter? Of course it fucking matters." Ros hadn't moved.

"She's my godmother," said Molly.

"Cara's nice," said Issy. "Poppy's a bit weird, though." A strand of linguine drooped from her mouth. She sucked at it and wiped her chin with the back of her hand.

"Christ." Ros dropped into her chair, her forehead in her palm.

"Have you seen her lately?" asked Diane softly.

"Uh," Issy shrugged. "I don't know."

"We saw them a few months ago," said Molly. "At Dad's."

"Well, that's fucking perfect," said Ros.

"Calm down." Peter held the bottle, looking for Ros's glass.

Ros fetched it from the floor by the window seat. "No, I won't fucking calm down. Poppy—" She held out her glass.

"Just wait," said Peter.

"I can't believe Harold's been seeing them behind my back."

"Not really behind your back, though, is it?" said Diane.

"He didn't want you to know," said Molly.

"I bet he didn't," said Ros.

"But he said I had a right to see my godmother."

"What's happened to her, anyway?" said Issy.

"Fuck," said Ros.

"Oh dear," said Diane.

"Fuck, fuck, fuck!" shouted Ros into her hands.

"Mum swears too much," said Issy.

"I'll handle it," said Peter.

"Can I have more sauce?" asked Issy, passing her plate.

He didn't use the word *suicide*. He said *accident,* like Cara's mother had. Issy cried and Molly went pale and pushed her plate away. Diane took them to the sitting room to curl under a blanket and watch old episodes of *Made in Chelsea.* Peter and Ros were left alone.

"Do you know what happened?" Ros watched her brother clear plates.

"How she did it?"

"No, I mean, why. Twelve-year-olds don't kill themselves."

"She was nearly thirteen."

"It doesn't make any difference."

He stacked the dishwasher, running each plate under the tap before loading them. "Something to do with being bullied, apparently."

"Did you speak to Cara?"

"Ben rang me."

Even hearing his name, even in circumstances like these, sent a jolt through her. "She was being bullied?"

"They think there was some YouTube video going around. About a girl in America. Same age. Same thing. They think maybe it was a copycat, an accident, you know? She won't have really understood. She was getting bullied and they think maybe she just thought she'd, I don't know, get attention or something. They don't think she meant to do it."

"Cara gave her too much attention."

"Ros. That's not fair." He wiped his hands.

Diane came back in. "They're settled. Poor things. Such a shock." She got out the Tupperware.

"You know what I mean," said Ros.

"About what?" asked Diane, transferring the leftover bolognese.

"Nothing." Ros put the Parmesan in the fridge. "So, when is it?"

"When's what?" Peter picked up the empty Le Creuset and put it in the sink. He turned the hot tap on full pelt and squeezed washing-up liquid into the water.

"The funeral. When is it?"

"Saturday."

Ros picked up her phone. "Which Saturday?"

"This." He started washing the pot. "The 23rd."

She opened her diary. *Saturday 23rd, BLITHE SPIRIT UP!* She sat down, refilled her glass, lit a cigarette and stared at it again.

19

DRESS REHEARSAL

It was one of those clear November days when winter seems worth it, when the sky is the exquisite blue of a Caribbean sea, the ground frosted and robins hop on spindle legs. The horses stamped and clattered against flint, the tractor churned up mud and fumes with hay bales in its teeth, gate latches pinched at frozen fingers. Clare put on an extra layer of tights beneath her jodhpurs, made breakfast silently, watched her daughter go off to school, curls bouncing against the fur-lined hood of her parka jacket, down the stony farm track to the lane, heard the bus aching to a stop to pick her up. She was full of Ros this and Ros that; *Ros lets Molly smoke, Ros knows Emma Watson* and, last night, *Ros says I can go skiing*, resulting in a row about money. It wasn't fair and it wasn't right and, to top it all, tonight was dress rehearsal.

At least she knew her lines, unlike Scott who relied on Issy to prompt him. Issy should play all the parts. She knew them better than anyone, even Ros who'd said, *Are we off book?* at the first rehearsal way back in October and assumed, when everyone had looked at her like she was mad, that they didn't understand theatre speak.

"Brian has his lines written on a coaster," Scott had replied, making Ros gasp and punch him softly on the arm. Clare had noticed everything. Right from the beginning. She led her eleven o'clock hack up muddy bridleways clogged with brambles, shouting over her shoulder, *Low flying,* when branches made them crouch to their horses' necks, and saw Ros everywhere. Ros shrugging out of her coat, a fur-lined collar like Nancy's. Ros getting parsley stuck in her teeth and pushing her bowl away. Ros saying, *She's lucky to have him.*

She'd always said to Tessa, *Your fracture lines make sense,* when Tess would complain, when Tess would cry, when she'd wonder why Scott stuck it out or she did. Theirs was a marriage of inconvenience, held together with common bounds; the war zone of his childhood, the war zone of hers. His might have been grenades and car bombs and Molotov cocktails thrown over the playground wall, but at least the violence was on the outside. Hers might have been floral pelmets and sparkling surfaces, but constant attack made more deadly by its hiding had shattered her equally and come out in the automatic weapon of her illness. Both had lived a childhood of threat. Both were running. Both found humour in the dark.

She texted Ros, *u coming tonight,* then felt stupid. Of course she was coming tonight. Ros hadn't missed a single rehearsal, she was hardly going to miss the dress. It was just that she hadn't heard from her in a couple of days. It was just that she couldn't help it. But there wasn't time to *delete for everyone* and anyway that would throw up an alternative awkwardness, so now she was going to have to live with it until she'd put the horses out and had five minutes to herself, which was never. They clattered into the yard, toes frozen, the line behind her crowding to a stop at the rails. Jump down, shin pain onto hard ground, horses knocking and rubbing, Clare took off her gloves and stuffed them in her pocket to undo soft noseband and cheek strap; the stable girls crowding, too, to help the novices untack. Her phone in her back pocket as she left them to it, a few strides to the tack room, she made coffee at the cheap tan kettle, the mugs on the sideboard stained, the teaspoons tide-marked, the Nescafé almost empty. Ros hadn't looked at her phone since 10:53 this morning.

Clare took her cup of coffee into her office, the tiny room off the tack room that was more paper than desk. She shut the door. She wanted to punch Scott. If it wasn't for Freddy and Tessa, she'd go and find him right now in his stupid zebra Land Rover and punch him right in that annoying swarthy face of his. He should know better. She looked at her phone. Nothing. She typed *want to get a bite before rehearsal?* And pressed send before she could stop herself. Now there was no way she could change it. One deleted message was a mistake, two were a story.

*

By the time Clare pulled up outside the theatre that evening, she'd looked at her phone fifteen times, and not looked at it twenty. She pushed the heavy green curtain aside to find the chairs had been put out and Brian already in costume, a heavy woollen suit, dark green – she was pretty sure it had been used in a performance of Robin Hood. He'd been supposed to wear a tweed suit suitable for an old Edwardian doctor shoved into the 1930s, but even Clarice the costume woman hadn't been able to make it fit.

"Ruth!" She'd been Ruth for over a month, even on the yard when he delivered hay bales. A couple of the new

DIYs had assumed that was her name and started calling her that.

"Sorry I'm late." She headed backstage, the door beside the kitchen that led to a small maze of corridors and rooms. In the girls' changing room, she found chaos, and Clarice, with pins in her mouth. Diane was trying on a tiara, a feather boa trailing; Issy was on her phone; a between-the-wars housemaid playing Candy Crush; while Barbara, sweating in worsted twill, tried to do up the buttons of a jacket three sizes too small. Between rails and mirrors, Clare looked for Ros.

Clarice, ancient and paper-thin, held up Ruth's costume, a black-and-white dress with sailor's collar for Act One. Acts Two and Three would be spent in a skirt suit last used by Tessa to play Nanny McPhee. That was when Tessa had been well, the clear water she'd hit that they'd all prayed would last, a handful of years of no nonsense, of meds and steadiness, though Tessa had said she was dying. *What more do you want?* Clare had asked her and she'd said, *To feel alive.* Clarice had already bull-clipped the back of the suit jacket to make it fit. Apparently it would be fine as long as she faced forward.

"Ladies," bellowed Brian from outside the door, rapping on it for good measure, making them all shout *Coming* and *For fuck's sake* and *Brian* simultaneously.

"He's like a bull," said Diane, discarding the tiara in favour of a sequined headband.

Clare shoved out of her clothes in a corner of the room, her heel stuck in the narrow jodhpur leg, mud from behind her knees scattering as she pulled it out. She was the last to get on stage.

"Announcements," said Brian, reversing into an armchair. The stage was set for the Condomine's living

145

room; a fireplace and armchairs, a mantelpiece and lamps, a piano made of plywood. There were art-deco ashtrays and occasional tables, one set with crystal glasses that caught the light – a mid-war, middle-class cosiness imagined from episodes of *Poirot* and *Miss Marple*. Clare had pointed out once to Brian that not everyone had the exact era of furniture in their house – she had a washbag from the 1990s – but Brian had told her in so many words not to worry her pretty little head, and Clare had reminded herself that am-dram was as much for the players as it was for the audience. It had nothing to do with real. Very little did.

Issy would make her entrance upstage, a doorway that doubled as an exit for all of them. Ros would appear through the glass doors stage right as if spiriting in from the garden. Clare would spend a great deal of time on the sofa. Brian put his hand down to steady himself. "As you all know, we're missing Ros tonight. Clarice is going to stand in for her."

Did they all know? Clare sidled up to Diane and whispered, "What's happened? Is she all right?"

Diane gave her an indeterminant nod and gentle pat on the arm that could have meant anything.

Brian continued, "Tech tomorrow, let's be on time, a lot to get through." He looked at his watch, fat and cracked on his wrist, and then at Clare. Clare pretended to itch her foot.

Scott already lounged in the armchair nearest the fireplace, an imaginary scotch in his hand in a not-imaginary glass. "Can I smoke?"

"We've been through this, Scotto." Brian pulled at his waistcoat, trying to stretch it over his belly.

"They all smoked," said Scott, miming a cigarette.

Lounging there like all the world owed him. Clare took her first position without catching his eye. She wasn't supposed to be pissed off with him until Act Two, but there was no harm in taking a run-up. Brian reversed into the wings, giving Clare and Scott the stage. They'd been through the fact that Noël Coward began with only Edith and Ruth – Issy and Clare; a comical conversation, mistress to maid, with Scott making his entrance mid-scene, but Brian had insisted that he knew better than the author, that the stage was too empty without Charles, that the audience expected it. Likewise for Ros, no disembodied voice from behind the fireplace for her, Elvira's entrance would take place entirely, and immediately, from the garden. Clare had whispered to Ros, *Seriously, don't bother, you should have seen his interpretation of Waiting for Godot. Who knew there was a talking bird?* and Ros had had to run off stage to empty her bladder. The good old days last month. When they were all friends and Scott hadn't done his crinkly eye routine and Ros called her almost every day. She went through the motions of her scene, Issy genuinely funny as the maid, haphazard and bobbing, almost dropping the tray, careering over carpet, running from her exit and suddenly they were in it, like magic the words appeared in her mouth as the scene unfolded, the Bradmans arrived and the lights were dimmed for a séance.

Or would be dimmed. Tech tomorrow, their tech man absent tonight and so they faked it, Brian filling in the change of gels and spots with verbal queues as if they all weren't a thousand times aware of it.

At the end of Act One, Scott caught her by the drinks table. "You alright there, Clare?"

She was tired of everyone making his life easy. Poor Scott. Mad wife. "I suppose you know why Ros isn't here."

Diane righted the stool she'd knocked over, Barbara straightened the rug.

"Why would I know?"

"Positions Act Two, everyone." Brian clapped his hands.

Clare raised her eyebrows and took up her pose by the mantelpiece.

When Clarice had a coughing fit, Diane filled in for Ros instead and tore her boa in the process, leaving feathers all over the stage. Brian forgot his lines and blamed the lack of lighting, Issy stole the show with double takes worth a Golden Globe and Scott delivered his performance of Charles as if the last months of rehearsals had been a complete waste of time. How did he do it? His natural ability was irritating. While Barbara helped Brian tidy props for the final act, Scott cornered Clare by the piano.

"Time of the month, is it, Clare?"

"Fuck off." She shook her arm free from where his loose grip touched it.

"Come on, you've a face like a slapped arse. What is it?"

"It's nothing."

"Well, if it's nothing, I was wondering if you could do me a favour."

If she was straight, she might have fancied him. His suit fitted perfectly, a deep-grey whorl, double-breasted and open to a shirt, the tie loosened. A mess of honey hair that he promised would be combed for opening night, those damned green eyes. Ros wasn't the first to feel seduced by him.

"You know, she's not as tough as she looks," she whispered as Brian said, *Nearly there, troops.* "She's fragile. You can't take advantage of her."

"Take advantage of who?" He moved to the sofa.

She sat beside him. "You know who, Scott. She's delicate; she's been through a lot."

"Are you talking about Tess?"

Clare laughed. "Yeah, right, your long-suffering wife."

"I'm perfectly aware she's delicate."

"I'm talking about your other wife."

"Ruth," shouted Brian from the wings, "less chit-chat, more spit-spat."

"What the fuck does that mean?" said Scott.

"You're holding up the scene," said Diane behind them. "It's Arcati and Charles."

Clare didn't answer. She got up and left them to it.

*

Later that night, far from the theatre and on her way home, she felt her phone buzz in her pocket. On the darkened road, she pulled over, a muddy gateway, not enough room but she found she couldn't wait.

u around tomr?

The thrill of it, the twist in her stomach, the lurch in her heart. She replied, *picking up Tessa then straight to tech. See u there?*

Silence. The three dots that taunted her. She looked up to waste time, the tangle of hedgerow lit by her headlights, the ping that made her look down again.

she's coming home?

Smiley face *yes*

Nothing. Last seen at. Silence.

20

RELEASED

The change in her meds caused a staggering veer in direction. The concrete hat was replaced by something tight around the temples, like the cap her mother used to wear for golf that made her face green and left the crown of her hair exposed. Not enough protection. Too much plastic. She rang Scott from the payphone and told him she needed her Australian leather Bushman that she kept in the wardrobe, the one with the wide rim that could be pulled down low, that offered cover on all sides. She shuffled to her goodbye meeting.

Dr Patel had her file open. She wore her glasses on a chain. "If the new medication is too much, we can swap to an anti-anxiety again, but we have to look out for a rash."

We. It wasn't Dr Patel who felt like she was wearing a golf visor. Dr Patel wore neat shirts with small flowers and her hair was combed and she was the nicest psychiatrist Tessa had ever met, but she still hated her.

"Finding the right medication at the right dose is a joint operation." Glasses jangling at her chest getting caught in the lapels of her jacket as she got out of her chair and held the door for Tessa. Tessa replied what she always replied, that she could do with a joint if she was offering. It landed with a tight smile and ache into the corridor where nothing waited for her but the lounge. She felt like she'd been run over by a truck leaking opiates and amphetamines; too fast and too slow, a complexity that was easier to achieve than it was to force someone to love you, someone who'd loved you once but didn't anymore. Her system throbbed; her eyes felt lopsided. Images of her outside life were beginning to filter through to her every day; a home to run, a son to care for, a husband who wanted his dinner. She didn't feel ready for any of it.

Clive patted the arm of his chair and motioned at the empty armchair opposite, as if Tessa was late for that appointment, too.

She picked up a magazine. "Where's Derek?"

Derek's chair had the frightening look of death; it may as well have had a sheet pulled over it. Clive had said any number of times that they'd be needing a plaque, more park bench than last resting place, but, given the stains, Tessa wouldn't be surprised if he'd died in it.

"Careers advice. He's talking about going back to work." Clive looked small without his friend, even smaller than with him. His chequered shirt and stonewash jeans decided on in the eighties, as if he'd forgotten to grow up but his face hadn't.

"Dr P said the C-word."

"Fuck me," said Clive, looking at the ceiling.

"She said they were letting me out in time to buy presents."

In the corner by the yucca plant, Ethel wailed.

Clive leaned forward. "Keep your voice down, pet." And they both looked at Ethel again. Last week, she'd got hold of a pair of scissors and cut the yucca plant's leaves into the shapes of animals. Derek had pointed out that if she'd been at the Tate, they'd have called it groundbreaking and put it in the Turbine Hall, but Ethel had been chastised and banned from the lounge, the scissors taken away from her, someone had got a bollocking. When she'd returned, no one had been able to get near the plant, Ethel stroking each leaf in turn, a cat, a giraffe, a monkey; she said they were her friends.

Roger had gone. Carrie had been moved to Worthing. New faces took up their places, unaware that that's where Roger sat, or Carrie twisted cotton on her finger, attachments and breakages that left those who stayed behind reminded of the futility of growing used to anything. Everything moved on except the illnesses they carried, these unwanted guests that moved with them.

"I remember a few years ago," Clive searched his pocket for cigarettes that weren't there, "a nurse put up tinsel by the serving hatch."

"Fuck's sake," said Tessa.

"They had to spray the room with Dettol. Get the stench out."

Everyone knew you didn't mention Christmas.

"You going home, then?" He itched his thigh, looked at Derek's empty chair, then at Tessa.

"Thursday." Pointless naming a day of the week. Today could be Thursday or Saturday or Tuesday. Nobody knew and nobody cared, but being given your ticket out was like being picked for the Hunger Games, ticked off one by one. "He'll be back soon."

"Oh, yeah." Clive nodded vigorously. "You know he has a PhD from York? Last time they took him back, he wrote a paper on climate control and what we can learn from the headhunters of Borneo and promptly fell down the stairs when delivering it to his head of college and the next thing they knew he was teaching classes without his trousers on. He's always said the trouble with the Western world is too many clothes."

"He's got a point," said Tessa, remembering the pond.

"He's got a lot of points," replied Clive and his hand drifted out and stroked the arm of Derek's chair.

Stewed fruit tea, smoking in the courtyard, weeds and damp, something terrible for dinner, was it chilli con carne or soup, impossible to tell, everything tasted of stale cigarettes and salt. A poor excuse for a duvet, a night spent waiting for the Diazepam to kick in, a morning spent sleeping and Nurse Ratchet banging on her door telling her to get up, her friend was coming at four. How to pack when she hadn't packed in the first place, T-shirts and leggings thrown into a bag six weeks ago that Scott had grabbed, a different dressing gown brought in later, her hairbrush and slippers. She didn't want any of it. It stank of institution. She picked up the holdall that had been bought for Freddy's sports kit, that had ripped the time he'd caught it in the car door and ripped more when Tessa had tried to grab it out of Scott's hands the time he'd packed it for her, and she hadn't seen the ambulance until it was too late. She took it to the lounge and emptied it on the floor in front of Ethel.

Derek, his chair an arm hug around him, Clive happier beside him, but the lounge felt empty anyway. It went like that in these places, the ebb and flow of bodies and troubles, the getting better, the falling ill again. They watched Ethel scrabble about in Tessa's underwear and socks, find her bathrobe and relieve it of the belt which she tied around her own waist to add to the three already there. The rest of Tessa's clothes she hung on a chair and bared her teeth at anyone foolish enough to come near. Tessa's hairbrush she secreted into the folds of her cardigan.

"Don't think about it," said Derek, looking away.

Tessa wondered if she tied four belts around her waist and bared her teeth they'd let her stay, too.

"You take care of yourself now, love," said Clive, his eyes on the clock. "Think of us."

"Did you get an exit visa?" said Tessa.

Derek blew his nose. "They're giving me till Friday to decide if living in supported housing fits with my life skills."

"That's tomorrow," said Tessa.

"Next Friday," said Clive. A lot could happen in a week.

A new patient with hair sticking up like a hedgehog wrote his name in pencil on a badge, stuck it to his jumper and turned his chair to face a circle that wasn't there.

"Keen," said Derek. Last week's group therapy had ended with her in the corridor, unable to fathom how she'd got there. They'd be lining up their chairs by the time Clare arrived.

"Maybe we could swap identities." She imagined Derek and Clive in her kitchen, Derek and Clive kissing Scott, Derek and Clive living the life of a woman who was supposed to be normal.

"Keep the faith," said Derek, blowing his nose again.

*

Sunlight glanced over her shoulders as she emerged from the sliding glass doors, an odd walk to the car, her feet unused to shoes, her hair unused to elastics; at the last minute, Ethel had crawled out from beneath the yucca plant and given her a French plait as if she'd never eaten a book or turned over a

154

chair in her life, as if she didn't wear three cardigans. Derek had said, "She used to work at Vidal Sassoon," and stood by it till Clive pointed out that there was a time when her daughters used to come, twin girls, to see her, and they must have been small once, they must have been children off to school. Ethel had kissed the top of Tessa's head and crawled back to her animals. Derek had given her his sunglasses, aviators from the nineties – they were only slightly too loose. A coat that Clare brought for her, puffy and white, stained, the zip broken, she'd meant to throw it away with the kitchen. She climbed into Clare's Subaru and hunched in the front, too big for the seat, too hot for the air but there was comfort in it, too; straw and mud, the smell of outdoors, Styrofoam cups crushed on the floor, a wrapper from the garage, *Wild Bean Café* – Clare had been at the sausage rolls again. Her life so simple, so unadorned with make-up or agony; maybe she could swap places with her instead.

"Have you got my hat?"

"I've got your hat." Clare passed it to her from the rear seat and put the engine into gear. Tessa blew straw from its brim and put it on. They veered out of the car park and slowed for an ambulance pulling into the drop-off outside the main hospital. She felt Clare look at her.

"It's going to be all right."

Was it, though? *All right* felt like a holdall for mediocre, and *it* could mean anything.

"I've made you a curry for supper. It's tech tonight; Barbara's picking up Freddy. I'll come by tomorrow, okay?"

"I want to come." She didn't want to be left alone.

"Barbara's waiting for us at yours."

"She brought me the script."

"Who brought you the script?"

"There's no kiss in it, Clare."

Clare slowed at the roundabout, her face busy but Tessa always knew when she was lying. She'd pinch her lips, scratch the edges. She'd lied about not fancying a woman at the stables; she lied about being gay, even though everyone knew except Ros who probably couldn't imagine any woman fancying another woman unless it was her they fancied. She didn't know why Clare hid it. Clare always said, *It's not secret, it's private, there's a difference.* She scratched her mouth now and Tessa looked out of the window.

Last time Scott had come in to see her, she'd known instantly, the scent of Ros all over him, an animal difference. She'd asked him, *What's happening?* and he'd said, *It's just a play, Tess. Let it go.* Ethel had eaten most of Act One, but Tessa had retrieved enough to know that they were never supposed to touch.

"Tell her to bring Freddy." She could be forceful when she wanted to be.

Clare sighed, indicated left and with her other hand rang Barbara.

But what was she thinking, really, as she climbed from institution to theatre hall, a dusty and cold cavern of a place, a stage on which Brian struggled with lights, shouting into the dark as spots beamed on and off. She sat at the back, a chair scraped from the row, little attention given, Clare already disappeared into the role of living wife. There, her husband, Tessa's, and Ruth's, she saw him put his hand to his brow as if on a ship, searching the darkness for her, she saw Clare whisper something in his ear, she felt with sudden heat the rush of her son's body as he launched from heavy green curtain into her arms. Freddy. He smelled the same.

But where was Ros? She waited and they waited, and Diane appeared to be playing two parts and then Clarice, paper-thin, spent half an hour pretending to waft in a doorway. Clive had done it better. She missed him.

21

FUNERAL

Molly made herself toast. Issy poured Shreddies. Ros sat in the garden, smoking her third cigarette of the morning, drinking her second cup of coffee, her feet up on a rotting chair, moccasin slippers and leg warmers. She'd banned the girls from owning UGGs. She had a scarf on, too, and her ski jacket over her dressing gown. It was freezing. Her breath made clouds, her cigarette smoke drifted over a garden hard-tipped and white. She glanced at the kitchen window and saw Diane kiss Issy on the head and Molly point at the back door.

"Only me." Diane wore a puffer jacket that could have doubled as a duvet. Full-length. Black. She'd zipped it to her chin, and around her neck she'd wound a pink pashmina for good measure.

"Have you got coffee?"

"Molly's making me some." She pulled out a chair and wiped the seat with her leather-gloved hand.

"They're damp. And that one's rickety." Ros pointed at another.

Diane sat down. "Are you okay?" She unwound the pashmina so that her lips were visible.

Ros shook her head. "Not really."

"The girls said they made you breakfast."

"I told them not to bother."

"They're worried."

Ros looked at her phone. "They have to get to school."

"Peter will take them. It doesn't matter if they're late."

"Molly's refusing to go."

"She's upset."

"I could fucking kill Harold."

"It's not his fault, Ros. Ah." Diane smiled up at Issy, who'd come out with a cup of coffee for her. "Thank you, my angel."

Issy plonked herself on her aunt's knee. "Molly's not going to school."

"She's had a shock, darling," said Diane, stroking Issy's head and tucking her blond hair behind her ear.

"I've had a shock, too," said Issy, shaking her hair loose again.

"You didn't know her," said Ros.

"Yes, I did," said Issy. "I want to go to the funeral."

"Don't be ghoulish," Ros replied, picking a stray piece of tobacco from her lips. She'd started smoking roll-ups. They felt healthier.

"Molly's going."

"No, she's not."

"I want to see."

"It's not a spectator sport."

"It's not for children," said Diane at the same time.

"How can a child's funeral not be for children?" asked Issy.

"Stop it." Ros stubbed her cigarette out on the edge of her chair and threw the butt into the roses, which needed deadheading.

"It wouldn't be right, darling," said Diane, gently. "And really it's only for close family and friends."

"Then why is Mum going?"

"Your mother was her godmother, Isswizz." Diane patted Issy's back.

"If Molly's going to the funeral, then I want to go the funeral."

"No one's going to the fucking funeral," shouted Ros, slamming her hand on the table.

"You are," said Issy.

She imagined it; the morning of packing, her suitcase containing black, her hair tied back, tissues in her bag. She imagined getting changed at the hotel, mascara waterproofed and lips muted, looking at herself in the mirror, getting into Peter's car, being driven in slow, silent arcs to the crematorium. She saw straggling clumps of people in hats, coats wrapped against cold, Cara's mother breaking away, the awkwardness of seeing Ben, the pain on Cara's face. There was the coffin arriving. There was Ben waiting to lift it to his shoulder, there were the pews filled with family and friends. She imagined not knowing where to sit. She imagined not knowing what to say.

"Go back inside, Issy. Get ready for school, there's a good girl." Diane tipped her off her knee. To Ros, she said, "And you're not to worry about the play."

Ros had been staring at the sky. A flight of geese in a perfect V had come squawking and harping over the park wall and landed in a field beyond the garden. "I'm not closing the play."

"Actually what I meant was—"

"What have you told Brian?"

"Clarice did a perfectly decent job of it." They spoke over each other.

"Molly says I'm allowed to go if I want to." Issy stood at the back door, her rucksack over her shoulder, her brown

160

duffel coat open over her school uniform; grey blazer with purple piping, trousers because she refused to wear skirts, sparkly winged trainers on her feet.

"Take them off," said Ros.

"Issy, aren't they *glorious*!" Diane clapped her hands.

"Dad bought them for me."

"Take them off," said Ros again.

"Is she not allowed to wear them?"

"What do you think?" snapped Ros. "And I'm not having Clarice take my part."

"Clarice is too old to play Elvira," said Issy. "Mum's *old* but at least she's not as old as Clarice."

Molly appeared behind her sister. Straight brown hair loose about her shoulders, a fringe she'd come home with that Nancy had cut for her, the kind that would look crazy on anyone over twenty, slightly jagged and slightly too short; you'd sue your hairdresser, yet on Molly, who had the magic all seventeen-year olds possess, that no amount of kale and yoga will give back to you, it was beautiful. Gold-rimmed glasses that she'd seen James Dean wear. Harem pants and tie-dye shirt, layers of loose cardigan and shawl; a cracked-up librarian in India, that's what Ros had called her the other day to much hilarity to no one but Ros. Molly put her hands on Issy's shoulders. "Why doesn't Issy play Elvira? You know everyone's lines, don't you, Iss?"

"Rehearsals are *so* boring," said Issy.

"Don't be ridiculous," said Ros. "A thirteen-year-old can't play Elvira."

"But I do," said Issy.

"No, wait, I think it's a good idea," said Diane. "Edith's much easier to replace."

"All I do is run about and say, *Yes, Mum.*"

"You do a very funny turn with a tray," said Diane.

"Got to get your kicks somewhere," said Issy.

Diane barked a laugh. "Heaven. Now, run along. Change that fabulous footwear. Such a shame. Go and find your uncle. He's waiting for you."

Issy kissed her aunt, ignored her mother, pushed past Molly and ran off into the house. They heard the front door bang.

"Now," said Diane, dropping her hands to her lap, "I think we have a solution."

"Issy's not playing Elvira. It's totally inappropriate."

"Even for one night?"

"She's thirteen."

"They can fluff the kiss."

"My dress won't fit her."

"Clarice can take it up. You're practically the same size everywhere else."

"And who'll play Edith?"

"We'll rope in Clarice for that. It'll be funny."

"I don't see how you can think anything funny right now."

"Ros, I'm not, I'm not." Diane laid her hand on Ros's knee. "You're in shock. We're just trying to sort things out, so you don't have to worry. Peter's been on to hotels in Bournemouth. He thinks if you leave first thing you'll have time to check in and change. Molly can stay with me."

"I can stay at Nancy's," said Molly. She turned on her heel and was swallowed by the kitchen.

"Or at Clare's." Diane finished. "And let me talk to Brian. All I told him was that there'd been a family tragedy and you were indisposed. Nothing more." She waved her hand across the space between them. "We can cover opening night and

162

if you don't feel up to it, we can cover the whole run, it won't matter a jot, and there's always next year. Why don't you go and have a nice bath and let me and Peter organise everything?"

Ros pushed Diane's hand from her leg. "No."

"What do you mean, no?"

"Sorry. I mean…" She lit a Marlboro. She still had half a packet in her coat pocket. "I mean, thanks, for everything. But I'd really rather deal with Brian myself. Is that okay? If I've nothing to do, I'll go mad."

Diane got up stiffly. She wrapped her pink pashmina about her neck. It pushed her hair up in a wave, an almost-black, dark-brown streaked with grey, Ros could never understand why she didn't dye it. In the UGGs Ros detested, she stamped her feet to get the blood flowing. "Of course. Of course you would. You do that then. And I'm sorry about tonight."

"What's happening tonight?"

"We've tickets for Hamilton. Been in the book for a year. Completely forgot until yesterday. Otherwise, of course, we'd have you all round for supper." She kissed Ros on the cheek. "Don't stay out here too long."

Ros nodded and sank lower in her chair, her jacket rose high on her neck. She zipped the front so that it covered her nose, sank into it as well; her breath felt hot in the small circulation of lining. Tessa would be home by now making coffee in the kitchen Ros had got to know, in the house she'd got to know. She'd be unpacking her things, having a bath in the bathroom Ros had cleaned when Scott had been out one night and not come back till an hour after closing. When he'd come in and said, *Sorry*, and invited her to come round for dinner the next night, just the two of them. Freddy was having a sleepover at school. He'd pretended he'd forgotten when she turned up at his door the following evening. He'd ruffled his honeycomb hair and said, *Shit, did I say that? Brian had me on the whisky. I must have forgotten,* and she'd said, *Not to worry,* and known that things said drunk are things said true, that he'd been unguarded, that he'd forgotten himself, not her. They'd said goodbye with a deal to meet at the pub after rehearsals on Saturday, last Saturday, and they had, and he'd kissed her, and when their steaks turned up, she found she couldn't eat and had given him half of hers as well. The rest of the cast hadn't joined them. They'd crowded at their usual table, Brian on the bench, Barbara being ballast at the other end, Clare on a stool and Diane in the only decent chair while Ros and Scott had disappeared into the alcove at a table in the other room, and Ros had almost said, *Shouldn't we go somewhere else?* but the range of his limbs had been so lovely. Also, he'd driven her there. She'd texted him *car won't start. You passing?* earlier that afternoon and he'd messaged *no probs* and sent a heart emoji.

Tomorrow, Tessa would be at the theatre, and Ros had never meant things to go this far. Tomorrow, Scott's living wife, who used to be her friend, who was her friend, would be taking her place in the audience, turning off her phone, hushing to a quiet and Ros was supposed to act normal. Why did these things always happen to her? Why couldn't she remember it was never *just* anything; a play, a favour, a man on his own, a wife out of reach and Ros, who listened, who always thought at the beginning that she was just trying to help. Ben, Scott, a repetition that made her feel put upon, a coincidence she put down to her own bad luck and unfailing allure plus the hopelessness of other people's marriages. She imagined the lights going up, Issy taking her place in a dress designed for Elvira, Scott without the real Elvira there to guide him. They hadn't spoken since Tess came home, not a text, not even a thumbs up; he'd had all day yesterday, but he hadn't even messaged to say *don't worry* or *we'll figure this out* or even *we need to talk*. She was freezing, she was stiff, everything hurt, but she couldn't bring herself to move.

22

HOME

It was a grey light that reached Tessa in the morning. Here she was with her family again, her husband and son. She looked across the table at Scott as he stirred his coffee. What did a man look like who'd been fucking someone else? She couldn't tell. She'd asked him last night, when he'd jumped down from the stage and come and found her in the dark, an audience of one, Freddy heavy with lolling head, all arms and legs, a ten-year-old made younger by sleep, *Are you going to leave me?* But he'd said, *I'm really tired, Tessa*, and lifted Freddy from her.

She said, "Do you want toast?"

Scott replied, "I'm fine."

Freddy sat sideways on his chair as if unable to commit to breakfast.

"What time will you be back?"

"Late."

"What about supper?"

"I'll get something after."

"After what?"

"The show, Tess. It's opening night."

She'd just wanted him to look at her. "What about Freddy?"

"Give him fish fingers."

"I mean, who'll pick him up?" She wasn't allowed to drive yet.

"He'll get the bus."

"I can walk on my own from the bus stop." A drop of milk spilled from his lips onto the table. "Ros says she used to walk home on her own when she was ten."

Her son, who now walked from bus stops on his own, who now put his bowl in the sink without being asked, skittered from the room in search of shoes.

Scott spoke quietly. He'd been halfway out the door, his hands patting for keys, tobacco, lighter, when he turned and came towards her, rested his palms on the back of the chair he'd been sitting in, stretched his fingers out, his wedding ring tarnished gold against the roughness of knuckles, hands that worked outside.

"If it happens again, I will leave you and I'll take him with me."

She'd thought it was Friday.

"You have to manage it, Tessa. You have to take your pills. Do you hear me? This is the last time."

She'd thought it was a normal school day, not a Saturday at private school when lessons carried on till lunchtime as if rich kids didn't deserve a weekend, a school her mother paid for, the anomaly of life carrying on outside as if they could have afforded the Priory but she'd been shoved in with Derek and Clive, Ethel, Richard, who, for all she knew, was the King of Spain, public psychiatric wards being the last stop for everyone.

"It's me and Fred, or it's this shite about not being ill. You've got to choose which you believe in. Dr Stemping says you can manage it, but you have to want to. You've got to come down to earth and listen to me because I'm not going through this again. You'll take your fucking pills."

But they made her head feel like she was crumbling.

"Are you sleeping with Ros?"

He picked up the chair and went to bang it down, but stopped short of the kitchen floor so that it banged against air and was replaced gently as he spoke quietly, "Do you think I've time for that?"

A quick ten-year-old hug that didn't last long enough, the possibility of an afternoon that stretched. She'd be expected to play games, watch a film, help him with his homework. She wondered as she listened to the slam of the front door, the pause before the crunch of tyres, whether he'd noticed she'd gone.

Day One of being home, the slow ache to recovery, the inexorable slide downhill and process of equalising as if coming up for air from the depths except it was the other way around. She'd been high and glorious; she'd forgotten to let go; she'd seen the ground fall away and then she'd fallen. Here she was, back on earth where her husband lived, and her son lived, and her house stood silent against the slanting rain. Here was Day One. Begin again.

She missed Derek; she missed Clive; fuck, she even missed Ethel with her sugar and twisting hands. She missed staring at the ceiling in her cubicle room and having nothing to do but sleep. She wiped a cloth over the ring of milk left by Freddy's bowl, the drops that had fallen from his lips. The coffee machine hissed and spat. She concentrated on getting the mug from its snug silver port. It was too hot, and the house was too loud and too quiet.

And too neat. The Aga had been polished and the work surfaces cleared of clutter. In the pantry, someone had turned all the jars round, labels to the front, and put the tins on the top shelf and the booze on the right. Drawers had been changed; when she went for a bread knife, she found string and Sellotape; when she went for a wooden spoon, she found cutlery. Even the utility room felt different with baskets empty, floor clean and washing powder, stain remover and fabric conditioner lined up in a neat little row on the shelf. None of it felt like hers.

You've got to grab it with both hands, Dr Patel had said and written down the name of a therapist. Grabbing it with both hands meant making a phone call, choosing a date, booking a taxi, getting dressed. She wondered, as she sat on the stairs, waylaid by a memory of water, if it was all a bridge too far.

There was a blank where change had happened; the man in the trilby, the police car following her, Scott's zebra-striped Land Rover running into the trees, a pregnancy that hadn't been real. Back here on earth, the regular, ticking life of her kitchen, her house, her family cast everything that had happened in the light of a brain in inexplicable meltdown. She couldn't trust anything of what she'd seen or heard, of what she felt then or now; she had no handle on truth at all. Except Ros. Except that feeling. But maybe she was wrong about that, too.

She experimented with going upstairs, standing in the bathroom that someone had cleaned, contemplated a shower in the cubicle that someone had mended. These people who called themselves healthy, who were allowed to walk freely while she was locked in a cage, were they so well? Were they so free of torment? They just hid it better; Clare with her secrets, Brian with his killer wrapped in tweed, Ros with her sashaying hips that made every other woman feel shit. Their symptoms didn't call the police, they were allowed to carry on as they were and when their torment spilled over in closed lips and anger and drunkenness, people called it privacy or duty or a laugh. People made allowances. All she was doing when she tore up the house was trying to make the outside match the inside, trying to live with her torment, too. Was it not preferable to pretence and bluster, to truth seeping out in stabbings so subtle it was hard to believe that they'd meant it? The secretive, the loud, the self-obsessed – where was the demand that they sort their shit out? They could sustain their habits, the public were on their side, they could have any drug they wanted. No one sectioned narcissists. They could self-medicate with booze and pot and sex, flashes of violence, arrogance and condescension, and everyone would say, *You shouldn't pry,* or, *He fought for his country,* or, *You know, Ros, she's an actress.* The emotionally dangerous could walk the streets freely, smashing lives. They'd been clever enough or lucky enough to stay this side of the line. Fools like Tessa had symptoms unacceptable – flooding bathrooms, wrecking kitchens, lying in a pond fully clothed. Who didn't want, even once, to take a hammer to a wall? Who didn't have the urge to throw their tea across the room? No one, that's who. Only the bipolar, the schizophrenic, the list of unacceptables suffered the ignominy of having their illnesses on full view and were punished to boot, locked up and given drugs they didn't want, drugs that made them cry, drugs that made them flatline.

Drugs that saved her life. That's what Scott would have said, and Dr Patel and Dr Stemping. She knew the door had swung off its hinges, she knew she wasn't capable of normal, but all she was trying to do when she ran wild was make the outside match the inside. *Play the game, Tess.* That's what

Clive had said as she was leaving. And Derek had added, *Send it my regards.*

She stood in the doorway of her bedroom that didn't feel like hers anymore, lay on the bed with her arms folded over her chest as if she were a saint in a catacomb. The disconnect had begun further back than she could remember, and she could only remember as far back as the cupboard under the stairs, her hammering fists, the taste of earth, her sisters whispering ways they were going to kill her. She remembered the uncertainty of walls, her burst into yellow light, the kitchen bright, her mother at the counter chopping carrots, the dog expectant at her feet. *They made me eat them* and her mother without stopping, *Wash your hands,* and there, a schism, a break in technicolour this time, not like the fine mist of her childhood before when she knew her parents were faking it, when unable to form the sentences, her brain told her this was wrong, no one was this happy, and if they were so fine what was that creeping sense of pain like smoke under the door? Could no one see it? A moment of tangible trauma denied to add to intangible years; her mother chopping carrots, *They only tease you because they love you,* her father enjoying the sunshine, the racing pages open, her sisters playing skip rope on the lawn and no one taking mind of her distress. A moment she was shooed away to do something else until a summer supper was ready, her tears ignored except to be told if she didn't eat her greens there'd be no pudding. There is no terror like the terror that your parents are lying; if those Gods can't be trusted, then what chance the world? And the fear that there were secrets to this game lay dormant, the cupboard closed and locked until, at twenty-one, on not enough sleep and too much speed, her brain had kicked it open so violently it had broken the hinges, yanked her into remembering with such force that she'd lost her mind. Outside had been a normal tinkly day, her sisters playing on the lawn, her parents lost in gin. Inside, she'd been screaming. She was still screaming now. As if she'd never stopped.

She didn't sleep but she almost did, a temptation of Valium pushed aside by another greater want. Opening night of *Blithe Spirit*, a week of performances, and months ahead of her own performance, the play called *Getting Better*. There'd be no applause for her; she was out in the world again where everyone was pretending. She was back on script, but psychosis had never broken them. They'd lived through worse, their honeymoon and Freddy. She wouldn't let a fake blonde with a 1930s voice break them now.

She called Scott.

"I want to come to the show."

Muffled voices, the sound of a chainsaw slowing.

"What did you say?"

"I said I want to come to the show."

She rang Clare.

"Can Nancy babysit?"

The scrape of shovel, the stamp of horses, her voice a little breathless. "We've got Moll staying at ours tonight."

Her phone beeped. She took it away from her ear.

The screen said *Ros*. And would she like to cut the call or hold, while, ten miles away, his ear defenders round his neck, Scott threw his phone on the seat beside him, got out of his zebra-striped Land Rover and slammed the door.

23   THE SHOW MUST GO ON

"Tessa?"

Tessa didn't answer.

"Tess? It's Ros. How are you?"

She sounded like she was outside.

"Clare said you were home." Pause. "Are you okay?"

What did she think? With her bouncing hair and tight ass, her perfect show at being friends with everyone.

"Moll can babysit, I think, if you want. She's staying with Nance, but they can both come. They can do their project at yours."

"Hi, Ros."

The sound of Ros breathing out. "So you're going to the play?"

In her head, she said all kinds of things. In her head she said, *If you're fucking my husband, you can fuck off,* but out loud she replied, "I'd like to see it."

They cut the call, both of them with a muffled apology for a bad line and someone else trying to get through and a few limp *great*s that didn't mean anything. Tessa felt sick.

She walked through her house and decided it wasn't hers; it belonged to a person with polished surfaces and

173

labels that faced the same way. She opened her wardrobe and saw clothes that belonged to a different her, a Tessa who'd thought white jeans were slimming. She lay on her bed in a room cold with the absence of Scott. Was he so well either? He shut his trauma away like Brian did, he refused his truth like Clare, he hid behind a persona of easy-going Irish like Ros with her fucking divorce martyrdom, an actress living it up in her role of stoic and generous while all the while keeping score, her eyes on the prize she made sure she could never be blamed for. Scott was a liar, too; they all were. He'd told her more in the first five minutes of their courtship than he had in the thirteen years since, a seduction of his war-torn childhood, the uncertainty of bombs, whose side he was on. The seventies in Belfast, and no matter what joke he made of it, his nerve endings hadn't laughed. They'd shored themselves up with a certainty that he wouldn't be afraid again and yet he'd married Tessa, a bomb on the nursery floor. *If it happens again, I'm leaving you.* But perhaps he'd already left.

She was staring at a Valium when Clare texted, *will drop girls over half five. Can give you a lift if you don't mind waiting? X.* After deleting ten other versions, Tessa replied *great, thanks, see you then xx.*

*

At five-fifteen, she still wasn't dressed and as Clare's Subaru drew up outside, Tessa changed from jeans to leggings again. Freddy had come in at just gone two, right about when she'd started worrying. They'd made pizza, or rather Freddy had shown her how he'd learnt to take it from freezer to bubbling, the unwrap of cardboard and plastic, the slide into the oven on the special cast-iron plate and, ten minutes later, out again all without burning his hands. She'd let him eat it in front of the TV and fallen asleep to the sound of gunfire. Her phone had woken her, a buzzing that said *sorry late on way now*. She saw, from her bedroom window, Molly say something to Nancy, who laughed as she shut the passenger door. All seventeen-year-olds looked the same, peachy and glowing. No amount of quinoa and Nutribullets would bring that back.

"We're here," Clare shouted up the stairs.

Tessa tried to remember how to arrange her face. She clumped down in black boots, the only ones comfortable after six weeks in slippers. Molly was tall, like her mother; a softer, more beautiful, brunette version of the woman Tessa couldn't get out of her head. She was sure they'd been friends once.

"I'll get Fred. Freddy," she called into the snug. "Come and say hi to the girls."

"We'll go and find him," said Nancy.

"Don't let him stay up past nine. And there's fish fingers in the fridge. And don't let him convince you he's allowed to watch *Family Guy*."

"Okay, okay, we won't," said Molly, laughing, as she followed Nancy into the TV room.

Clare gave her a hug. "You sure you want to come tonight? You feeling up to it?"

Why? How did she look? Like a mental patient on day release? "I'm fine." She looked for her bag and found it under her coat on an armchair in the sitting room. She couldn't look at the hat stand.

As she got into Clare's car, she said, "Nancy looks well."

"New pony. 15'2". A real goer. You should come and ride."

They slammed doors and did up seat belts. Clare's Subaru stank of the muck heap and straw, a leathery saddle soap that Tessa loved.

"So she's good, is she?"

"He. Tommy. She'll grow out of him, but he'll give her a summer and then we'll sell him."

"I mean, Ros."

"Oh." Clare bumped slowly down the rutted track that led to the main road. "Well, yes, of course, she's a natural. She was always going to be good. We're a bit lost without her."

"What do you mean, lost?"

"Her goddaughter died."

"Did she kill her?"

"Tessa!" Clare looked shocked. Normally, she'd have laughed. She checked left and right before pulling onto the main road.

"I'm just saying."

"I only heard about it from Diane last night. She was a teenager. Fucking awful. And Brian's going to hit the roof if he hasn't already, as if a play matters more than that poor child."

"Why?"

"Funeral today. She's in Bournemouth."

"So she's not in it?"

"Not tonight, she isn't. Issy's playing Elvira."

"They'll have to fluff the kiss then."

"That's what Diane said, too."

There was traffic going over the bridge, a bottleneck of cars that snaked all the way back to the BP garage. Tessa remembered a slam of breaks, Scott's face blank in the pale green light as he'd picked up a bottle of Jacob's Creek to take to that last summer party when they'd hoped it wouldn't rain. They inched forward, leaving the petrol station behind.

"But she's good. Ros, I mean, in rehearsals. She was good." Like a scab, she couldn't stop picking.

"She wiped the floor with us," said Clare, checking her rear-view mirror.

"Peter said she would."

"Have you spoken to him?"

"No, I mean, before." Tessa pointed her thumb over her shoulder as if last September was on the back seat, Peter and Diane's sunny garden, one lonely drumstick on the cooling barbecue, men gathered in tweed and rugby, Ros in heels and tight jeans. "He never wanted me to do it."

"Peter?"

"Scott. He always wanted her to do it."

"She didn't plan it."

Now that Tessa thought about it, she wasn't sure if Clare didn't look a little plastic.

They inched across the bridge. "Look, Tess, if I were you, I'd just…"

Tessa looked at her friend. She'd just what? Let him go? Accept defeat? High five Ros as the better woman? "You'd just what?"

"Nothing. Just get better." They were opposite the turning, waiting for the road to clear, indicating right as hybrids glided past. Clare accelerated in front of a Tesla bumped over the pavement, slowed into the theatre car park and drew up beside Scott's Land Rover.

People only say they're fine when to say anything else would take too long or make them cry. She'd already given the same reply to Barbara and Clarice, who'd come bustling in a minute after them. Now the tea ladies arrived and the ticket ladies were offering her a quick cuppa, the kitchen hatch open onto the stark Formica of catering. It would be shut for the performance. Tessa felt like a fool standing there in the theatre all alone among rows of empty seats. Clare had already whistled off into the bowels of the theatre to transform herself into Ruth. The echo of someone swearing and the clang of something hitting the stage made Tessa leave her coat on a chair and draw back a corner of the curtain. The Condomine's living room, a summer evening, the fire lit, there was the piano, the sofa, the mantelpiece, the glass doors to the garden stage right. Tessa thought of Clive. Ashtrays and books and standing lamps; a pre-war interior lit badly. Beside the occasional table, a stepladder rucked the edge of a rug. A screwdriver lay at its feet. She could see Brian's legs, the top of him obscured by lights.

"Balls." A red gel fluttered down and landed near the fireplace.

"Shall I get Scott?"

At the sound of Tessa's voice, Brian's face appeared, peering down at her through the crook in his arm. "Tessa!" He started down the ladder. "You're back." He reached the stage, looked up at the light again, then smiled at her. "How was Spain?"

"We're here, we're here," called a voice from the other side of the curtain.

"You don't look a bit tanned." Brian hitched the curtain back.

"Spain?" Tessa followed him off the stage.

Diane rushed down the aisle trailing scarves, with Issy behind her. "Traffic, traffic. Tessa!" She kissed her on both cheeks. "How lovely you're here."

"I was just saying she doesn't look a bit tanned," said Brian.

"Where've you been?" said Issy.

"Tell me about those lights, Brian," said Diane. "Did you fix that spot?"

"I think I need Scott to get up there again."

"I'll go and get him," said Tessa.

"I'll come with you," said Diane, taking her arm. "Issy, run along and find Scott."

They slipped into the corridor beside the kitchen where it was quiet. Diane made Tessa face her. "How are you?"

Tessa left Diane at the changing-room doors. The empty theatre felt preferable. Scott was already up the ladder when she faded into the blackness of the hall, the house lights still down. Brian, like a bull in a glass box, shouted orders from the lighting board. None of them saw Ros arrive.

The theatre filled up, the air became noisy with chatter, a queue for the bar, Tessa tried to stay calm. Say hi, smile, wave, keep everything to yourself. Scott might have mentioned that he'd told everyone she'd been out in Marbella looking after her parents. After the fourth time, she could almost believe it was true. Thankfully, the lights went down before she was tempted to embellish it further and the air rustled into reasonable quiet as the curtain lifted.

CURTAIN UP

Backstage at the theatre, the female members of the cast were jostling for position among the cramped clutter of their communal dressing room. Issy struggled with Kirby grips getting lost in her hair. She'd already dropped three down the back of her maid's outfit; a teenager in bob-cap, her phone shoved up her sleeve, her mother had tired of telling her, *If it falls out mid-scene, that's your problem,* to which Issy had not tired of replying, *Brian said it was a comedy.* Diane, dressed in more material than any of them thought possible, a silk scarf tied over her head, another round her neck, still more across her shoulders, couldn't decide between eight bangles and ten, while Clare wished she hadn't said yes to a tweed skirt suit and Barbara wished she had. Rails sagged under the weight of costumes past, hangers jangled as they were pushed aside, name tags tangled with coat buttons. On the floor, crowded with bags and their own clothes discarded, heels were knocked over and muddled, a white shoe dotted with imitation diamonds lay on its side, the lace of an Edwardian boot wound around a metal leg. A full-length mirror, white plastic frame, was propped against a wall, while the only table heaved with fake diamond earrings, tiaras and necklaces, fascinators with feathers tired, trays of make-up, lids off, lipsticks dented, mascaras dry, and blue boxes of pins and clips and hair bands, a brush that everyone had used. In among it all was Ros, feeling brilliant.

"Positions, *please*." Brian's stage whisper was louder than his real voice; they could have heard it in Petworth.

"The *curtain*," Brian finished as Clare flung open the door.

"So sorry." She ran past him, followed by Issy, who stopped mid-stride, returned to the dressing room, grabbed her tray and ran out.

Ros held her arms in the air as Clarice turned her around. "You've lost weight." She rouched the dress in handfuls at Ros's spine. "I don't know how many more times we can take it in."

"I can't seem to eat enough."

"You can't have nerves."

"A show's a show."

"It's a sell-out," said Clarice, taking a pin from her mouth.

"Is it?" She'd been longing to peek through the curtain, superstition had held her back, so much was expected of her, she didn't want to let the others down. Her dress, a waterfall of silver and satin, was a ghost of the thirties, and by far the most stylish of everybody's. One shoulder was bare, the other was draped in lace.

"Help," said Barbara, her face puce, her body wedged into screaming-green taffeta. Diane got up and fought with the zip, while Barbara clung to the wall.

Ros dropped her arms. "How's it look?" She was pretty sure it looked gorgeous.

She'd meant to get in earlier, give Clarice more time, but a certain fear had overtaken her, not fear, but Diane would never understand. Peter had shouted at her for a full hour or it had felt like that, standing in her kitchen this morning dressed in his mourning suit. *Don't you dare come over all Vivien Leigh with me. It's only a fucking play. She was your goddaughter. Cara was your best friend.* Was, she'd wanted to shout back, but hadn't. She'd had too much of a headache. Her voice had been plaintive. *I broke up their marriage* and he'd replied, *No, you fucking didn't.*

"It'll do for tonight. I'll have it fixed up for tomorrow." Clarice turned her around.

Ros tried on a glittering tiara.

"I don't think I can move," panted Barbara.

"We're on," came Brian's voice through the door again. Barbara waddled across the room.

Ros listened to the rise and fall of laughter from the auditorium, she knew the play so well, could tell when Issy made a performance of carrying drinks, when Barbara and Brian made their entrance. Diane was on next; she'd already said, *Break a leg,* and jangled from the dressing room to wait in the wings. Ros wasn't on until the end of scene two, her entrance in a voice perfectly charming and perfectly strange, she'd been practising on the dogs all week.

It was obvious she couldn't have gone; it had been obvious from the moment she'd seen *picking up Tessa.* Not that any of them knew that, at least she hoped they didn't, her and Scott had been pretty careful, and they hadn't explicitly talked about it, but it had felt as if they had so much time, she'd forgotten Tessa was ever coming home. For twenty-four hours, her ghoulish desire to be at the centre of a tragedy had fought with her deep craving for applause, and then along had come Clare's text, a fate sealed. There was no way she could leave his side now. Anyway, she thought, poking her head out of the dressing room, Ben and Cara wouldn't want to see her, and she knew how she felt about Poppy's death, too. She didn't want to be a hypocrite; *I told you so* wasn't going to help anyone. All of these judgements, these reasons piled up in Ros as she listened in the corridor to the round of applause that greeted Diane; what a good, amateur crowd they were, as if it was some sort of talent show. She let the door softly shut behind her. Had they never heard of the fourth wall? Apparently not.

She inspected her face, her hair, tried to see the back of her dress. When he'd rung her, she'd missed the call and when she'd rung him back, he hadn't answered. Then, pinging into WhatsApp, *T wants to know if M can babysit 2nite,* as if it was some sort of code for *play it cool.* Maybe he'd even told her already – a scream brought Ros to the door again. Madam Arcati had fallen off her stool and Elvira's cue was any minute, her voice that would waft in from behind the fireplace, the doorway, the window. Or was supposed to. She'd suggested to Brian they pre-record her disembodied lines and hide speakers about the set to create the impression of her moving invisible from place to place, and he'd said, *Right-o, Ros, I think we'll have you say your lines from here,* and positioned her stage left out of sight. She moved quietly into position, felt the heat of the stage, the breath of the audience, their bodies lost in dark. At least her and Scott were side by side on this, at least they could talk to Tessa together. She felt bad, but not that bad; it wasn't as if she'd planned it. Perhaps Tessa would understand that you can't abandon a man like that and expect life to carry on as normal, that chemistry was chemistry, that all of it had been inevitable. Maybe they could sit down after the show was over and figure it out like grown-ups. He could probably move in with her if he didn't mind the dogs.

"Leave it where it is." Perfectly charming and perfectly strange. How the others hurried their lines, how she waited until everyone was listening. "Elvira, of course…" The dead wife of Charles, the one more beautiful, more seductive, stepping into the light Ros ceased to exist in her other world; no dead goddaughter or ex-best friend, no inconvenient wife except the wife of Charles in the Condomine's living room and Dr Bradman staggering about with a whisky. There was Madam Arcati making too much noise, Mrs Bradman unable to get up off the sofa, Edith dropping her tray. She watched Ruth deliver her protests to Charles and Charles, ever handsome, see the ghost of the woman he loved, the woman he couldn't resist.

The heaven of it, the lift and warmth, the words that fell from her lips as if she had thought of them, how she moved as if impelled by the moment, a magic that overtook her. She looked out into the audience and saw the wall of the Condomine's sitting room, she drifted to the mantelpiece and felt the warmth of the summer fire, she saw Charles flick his lighter with shaking hand and caught the scent of Pall Mall cigarettes. A dream world enveloped her, time stood still.

Only the light change and applause at the interval brought her back, the curtain dropping, the others screaming in hushed tones, *Isn't it going well?* but Ros avoided all of them. She slipped away, no costume change for her, an upturned crate backstage, her composition held. *Stay in the space,* her drama teacher used to say. He'd never call it 'character'. Ros *was* Elvira, she was real.

And the play, which was real life to Ros, too – the story of two wives, one husband; two women caught up in the battle for one man's soul, swept along through the hours of bright lights and upturned faces. Her hand along the back of the sofa, the placid, silk exterior of her ghostly charm, the calm with which she made her case, her memories of being Mrs Condomine. In those hours that felt like years, she breathed and expanded and believed herself whole. Charles flung his arms about her. The kiss brought a squeal of protest from somewhere but Ros imagined it a bird outside – how many times had Brian argued that you can't kiss a ghost and she'd said she'd seen it at the Almeida and they'd got clean away with it there. It had added to the mystery of death; it had made the play fizz with the unexhausted passion between them; it had given substance to this thing called forever.

Applause, encore, hand in hand between Clare and Scott, they bowed three times before the others joined them. Issy got a standing ovation, but Ros forgave her; am-dram crowds were always kind to children. The curtain dropped and they rushed off stage, a clamouring of *darling!* and *sweetie!* as everyone hugged, their make-up streaked, their hair drooping. Brian mopped his brow. Scott clapped him on the back, the women crowded into their dressing room. She'd been fabulous. She'd been a fucking star.

"My darlings!" She held out her arms. "You were all wonderful!"

"One down, seven to go," said Clare.

"I forgot my lines," wailed Barbara.

"I fluffed an entrance," said Clare.

"Pub?" said Issy.

"Get a lift with Diane," said Ros, taking the only chair at the make-up table, a bottle of cleanser in her hand. Scott would be waiting for her, how she'd taken to always leaving her car at home, getting a taxi in, not bothering with excuses anymore.

But he wasn't there when she came out, so she was forced to walk.

It took her half an hour, she practically ran it, her coat hugged about her, her collar up. He'd held her like he never wanted to let her go, he'd kissed her with a look that said everything. She checked her phone. Ten to ten. The funeral would be over by now, the wake probably, too. She saw sandwiches curling on floral platters in Cara's mother's floral house. She saw the drifting away of last guests. They used to sit on the carpet and imagine drawing all over the walls, turning the prettiness to Borneo, the ruining of paintwork. Those pelmets and lace-backed chairs, how they'd laughed at all of it. No one would have been laughing today. It was odd that she didn't feel a thing. As she pushed open the door to the pub, she wondered if Poppy had been cutting herself.

Loud, warm, full of life, Brian roaring, Clare grinning, the pub opened its arms and swallowed her. She sashayed up to the bar.

"Elvira!" said Brian. "We thought we'd lost you."

"Where's Charles?" She put her bag on the floor and took off her coat. Diane looked at her once and went back to her conversation.

25   CURTAIN DOWN

She wanted to stab her in the face. She wanted to take that smug blonde look and scratch its eyes out. That fucking dress with the shoulder off, that voice as if she was Audrey Hepburn on a pub crawl, and who the fuck said it was okay to kiss a ghost. Tessa hadn't meant to squeal; it had come out, a noise like a pig stuck under a gate, like Ethel used to make in Mercury Ward when someone asked for sugar. She'd sat at the back, well out of sight, but she was still sure Ros had seen her. The curtain hadn't been dropped for five minutes before Scott came shooting out of his dressing room and scooped her up, the theatre still emptying when he pushed her into the Land Rover and clicked the door shut. She wasn't an imbecile. She could manage. But they rowed on the way home.

"I told you it was too early."

"Are you having an affair?"

"You should have stayed at home."

"If you're leaving me for her, I'm taking Freddy."

He almost drove into a ditch, taking the lanes too fast, another car head on, horn blaring, a screech to a stop, nose to nose.

"You need to get some sleep."

"Was it her who turned the jars around?"

She practically fell out when he stopped outside their house. She thought he was dropping her off, that he was going to screech away to the pub as soon as she slammed the door, but he sat there for ages, engine idling while she fiddled with her keys, tried the lock, was met by Molly already with her coat on, Nancy behind her. Of course. The babysitters. Molly, so like her mother, only not a bitch. He rattled off with them both squashed up in the front and she heard him moving about downstairs no more than half an hour later, not enough time to have gone anywhere but Clare's house. And when he crawled in beside her, he didn't stink of anything but whisky and regret, that scent of a marriage like smoke under the door, a smouldering degree shift taken some forgotten year ago when it hadn't seemed important; how a decade later they were miles off course.

"It's not my fault." She meant her illness. "Scott?" The rough mound of him immediately still. "I didn't ask to be ill." An owl outside the window, the bark of a muntjac in the woods. "You're not so fucking perfect yourself, you know." His snore – fake or real, she couldn't tell.

The week passed in a haze. She hardly saw anyone as, night after night, the Midhurst Amateur Dramatics Society took to the stage. Brian found excuses to touch Clare, Clare couldn't keep her eyes off Ros, and Ros lived for the moment when Scott took her in his arms. None of them wanted the show to end except Tessa who, night after night, suffered Scott coming home drunk, stinking of the stage, the pub, that fucking woman who used to be her friend. They hadn't spoken since the awkward call, not a text, nothing; it was as if Tessa had ceased to exist.

On Sunday, Clare came round and was weird. She sat in the kitchen talking about anything but Ros. After she left, Diane called to see if she was okay. Did all of them know? Was it all over the *Midhurst Gazette*? *Sexy Irish Fuckhead Goes Off With Woman Pretending To Be An Actress.* She could write the copy herself.

Ros wasn't the first. Women were always falling over themselves for Scott, incredulous that mad, fat Tessa could have landed a husband like him, all but asking, *How did you do it?* She knew they assumed it was the sex and it used to be wild, but that wasn't it. *You understand me, Tess,* that's what he used to say and, cosy beneath blankets, they'd laugh at the social-climbing, red trouser-wearing, dinner party-throwing Home Counties set. They'd say, *Thank fuck for you,* and hold each other tighter. But her illness had stolen everything; his desire, her faith, her agency to ask anything of him like not to drink so much, like to look at her once in a while, like to say anything other than a perfunctory *hi* and occasional *see you later.* That degree shift many moons ago when they'd first met; a pregnancy and an illness, their wedding bands already at the bottom of the Orinoco River, a honeymoon of reveal that they'd both washed over and imagined it was the stress of the wedding, her mother telling her she should walk down the aisle backwards – her dress looked so much prettier from the rear. How he'd persuaded her to laugh it off, how he'd charmed her mother, how her mother had tried to dissuade him, caught between her desire to have her daughter off her hands and her need to make her fail, how he'd said, *I'm no angel either*, and in the front seat of the Land Rover, driving away from lunch, they'd decided the only thing for it was to run away together. They should have; they should have got out of West Sussex and the ghosts that lurked at every corner for Tessa. There, the terrace where the marquee had stood, a celebration of her 21st birthday that she'd spent in The Priory while her friends carried on without her. Her father had said there was no point in wasting good champagne. There, the tree stump where she'd sat hour after hour rather than go back inside to the tinkling, sparkling kitchen; her mother chopping carrots, the dog's nails click-clacking on the scrubbed kitchen floor. There, the cupboard, the scratch of the brick while her father in sunshine turned pages of the racing paper and her sisters played skip rope on the lawn.

On Monday, she failed to hear the man from Ocado and he left, leaving them bereft of milk, fish fingers and butter. On Tuesday, a branch crashed onto the fence, narrowly missing Scott's car. On Wednesday, Clare came over again and instead of slagging Ros off when Tessa said, *It's not the fucking West End*, she defended her. On Thursday, Tessa burnt the soup and on Friday, she stayed in bed all day, unable to get up even when Freddy came in from school with a clay dinosaur he'd made her. On Saturday, Scott came home at lunchtime to give Freddy his tea; she heard them making lasagne together while she dragged herself from bed, down the waterfall of stairs, and lay in the sitting room staring at the blank TV screen. She heard the ping of the timer, the clank of the Aga door, Scott taking over despite Freddy saying he could do it. She heard Scott say, *Run in and get your mother.*

His little face so blond and sweet, those green eyes like his dad, a soft roundness that would surely fade and the thought of it made her cry inside, while outside she wondered how she'd find the strength to get up out of the deep feather cushions and follow him to the table. She wasn't hungry. She'd have to pretend to be, like she had to pretend everything else.

"Look at this." She sat down in the chair Freddy pulled out for her.

"I did all the chopping." Freddy sat beside her.

"And you grated the cheese." Scott cut slices. He eased one out with a spatula; tomato sauce and béchamel dripping, a courgette escaped back into the dish.

"It looks delicious," said Tessa, feeling nauseous. "We can play scrabble later." He'd asked her every day after school and every day she'd said, *Tomorrow.*

"Fred's coming to the show." Scott finished serving, took off the oven gloves and took his place opposite her. He picked up his fork.

Tessa was still in her pyjamas. She looked at the clock. "I need a shower."

"You're not coming."

"I want to come."

"You've seen it already."

"Then who'll sit with Freddy?"

"Molly and Nancy," said Freddy, separating his vegetables from the collapsing layers, the beef getting mixed with white sauce.

"Why didn't you tell me?" It was like a whole world was going on without her.

"I am telling you." Scott blew on a forkful of mince.

"And what about coming home?"

"I'm not going to leave him there, am I now?" He touched his son's cheek.

"But the after-party." There was always an after-party at the pub.

"It's tomorrow. Diane's throwing it at her house."

"Tomorrow?" Tessa had been planning on staying in bed.

"Yes, Tess, tomorrow. Is there a problem with that?" he said it sweetly, but he didn't mean it like that. He meant, *What of it?*

"And who's going to babysit tomorrow, then?"

"He can come," said Scott. "It's not like the world and his wife won't be there, now, is it? Eat up, Fred." He'd already cleaned his plate, a lasagne shovelled down, one eye on the clock.

"You're not leaving me at home for that." Tessa had hardly touched hers. The layers were congealing.

"What are you, five years old? You can do what you like."

"Then I want to come tonight."

But he was already on his feet. He was already shoving Freddy into his warm coat and holding out his boots for him to put on, he was already checking his pockets for his keys, and the door slammed before she had time to stand up. She wasn't sure if they'd even make it to tomorrow.

Scott and Tessa weren't the only ones feeling upset.

Ros crashed plates into the dishwasher. The euphoria of opening night had worn off. What the fuck was he thinking, asking Molly to look after Fred again? She wasn't a fucking monster. Once was enough, twice was totally inappropriate. It put her in a totally fucking shitty position. It was as if she was rubbing it in Tessa's face. They could at least have a semblance of decorum. But Scott was barrelling on as if no one's feelings meant anything to the greater scheme of his easy passage through life. Had he even spoken to Tessa? Had he said anything at all? And what the fuck was she supposed to do meanwhile? Just sit around and wait? Everyone would just fall into line, would they? Tessa would say, *You knew, and you still let Molly sit with him,* and Ros would feel ashamed. If or when it all came out, she at least wanted to feel like she'd done nothing wrong. And Peter and Diane weren't talking to her either.

Clare tripped over a bucket and caught her finger in the hinge of a stable door that slammed open in the wind. It was obvious what was going on and Tessa was her friend. She wished she could have nothing to do with Scott at all and she wished that just once in her life she could have the balls to go after what she wanted, to admit it, to be honest about her heart. Watching Ros field the passes of Scott's casual seduction only made her love her more. Fucking men. Ros felt even further away, not closer but taken by the attention of that man who should know better, who never tired of pulling the same trick – poor, handsome, Irish, psycho-picked Scott, worn-down husband, who everyone said, *He's so loyal, I don't know how he does it.* Clare knew how; it was like a single dad walking into a playground of mothers. It was as easy as shooting fish in a barrel. No one could tell her that he didn't like the pay-off. So what if he was good on stage? She couldn't look at him at all. She was too angry.

Brian was furious with the lights, which had burnt out three gels that week, and with Ros, who was needlessly out-acting everyone, and with Scott, who seemed to have upset Clare and not noticed. He watched them in the pub; Scott buying drinks and Clare saying, *I'll get my own, thanks.* If something had happened between them, he'd fucking kill him. Scott already had a wife and he had Ros rubbing herself all over him. He couldn't have all three. Clare, if she ever realised it, belonged to him.

Meanwhile, in bed last night, Diane and Peter had agreed that it was the last straw.

Even the weather found something to complain about; the wind whined through the trees, clouds crowded the sky in ominous iron grey and the sun fought back in fits and starts, sending rays of bright winter across trees stripped of leaves. It couldn't decide whether to rain or snow or brighten everyone's day with unexpected bursts of light. Everything felt like it was breaking.

26 THE AFTER-PARTY

Ros was woken by Issy drawing back the curtains.

"Jesus, Iss."

"It's midday."

"So?"

"We're hungry."

She buried her face in the pillow. A tinny, iPhone rendition of 'Private Dancer' filled the air. Issy chucked Ros's phone on the bed and walked out. Someone had put it on last night, too. She'd danced cheek to cheek with Scott until, over his shoulder, she'd caught Clare's eye like a warning, so she'd clung onto her instead and they'd swayed between tables, Scott watching from the bar. Diane hadn't come with them to the pub, thank God. She'd left the theatre with a wave and a *See you all tomorrow night. Come for seven. Bring a dish.*

She tried opening her eyes. What to wear, that was the question. What to wear to the after-party and how to tell Tessa that her marriage was over. She turned off Tina Turner and checked her messages; one from Clare, *you still standing?* They'd played that as well, Clare with her fists in the air, Brian stomping about like a demented soldier. She texted *just*, stumbled to the bathroom and turned on the ancient shower that a 1960s renovation had arranged badly. A circular rail like a *Star Trek* prop, a grey plastic shower curtain, she stripped off her Calvin Klein leggings and T-shirt. The slope of the claw-footed bath made standing directly under the stream impossible. With one foot flat against the end, she remembered for the millionth time that she needed to descale the rose, half the shoots shot water sideways. He'd said to her in a stolen moment, both of them smoking outside, *There's never a right time. If I'd walked while she was in, I'm a bastard. If I walk now, I'm a double bastard and if I wait till she gets better, she gets Fred.* She couldn't quite remember what she'd said in return, but it was something like, *I'll wait for you*, before Brian had come reeling out to join them. She'd staggered inside and draped her arms around Clare. Good old Clare. So dependable. So timid. So fucking nice. All night she'd wanted to shout, *Pick a fucking side*, but instead she'd listened to her go on about how much Tessa needed her friends.

She felt sorry for Tess, but not that sorry. It had been one long bitch from the moment she'd met her, nothing but complaints; Scott doesn't do this, Scott doesn't care about that. Ros scrubbed her armpits with a flannel. *Poor Tess*, that's what everyone will say. *Poor Tess*. Shampoo streamed down her face. What about *poor Ros*? It wasn't as if she'd pushed him. She'd been to hell and back, and how was she to know she'd meet her soulmate in the yellow-painted confines of West Sussex? She was only sorry she and Tess had become friends. She felt bad about that; if she'd known, she'd have kept well away.

*

Clare drew up outside Ros's house, as promised, at six. Always the good girl, never late, never letting anyone down. Just once she'd like to be like Ros and have people say, *Did you see?* Last night, Barbara had said, *Did you see the way she rubbed herself on him?* as if the real show was in the pub, not the stage they'd just left. *It's not right*, Barbara had added and gone off to find her coat as if sharing the scene had infected her. Clare slid the tray of vol-au-vents from the front seat and rescued the two bowls of potato salad from the boot. Her head hurt. And her heart. She didn't mind making Ros's food contribution, but she did mind never being allowed to touch her the way she wanted to; not as a prop for Ros's arms, not *what would I do without you?* slurred into her ear as 'Private Dancer' faded into 'Come On, Eileen'. She nudged the unlatched front door with her shoulder and edged sideways into Ros's kitchen, the cling film crinkling at her fingertips. Crosby and Nash jumped up to greet her, tails wagging. She dumped the food on the kitchen counter and patted their heads in turn.

"This is the last thing I feel like doing."

"Eating?" Ros stood at the small mirror that hung by the scullery door. She fixed her earrings; long, gold, dangly, a cupid firing an arrow.

"Going out."

"It's not really out."

"Well, it's not in, is it? I'd rather be in my pyjamas. How are you?"

"Like a pig shat in my mouth."

Clare laughed. She'd introduced her to *Withnail and I* one night huddled on her sofa while Nancy and Molly were off doing their Duke of Edinburgh and Issy was on a sleepover with a friend. A bottle of Shiraz, a bowl of popcorn and Clare's ancient DVD player. Clare had quoted all the way through, a rare moment of triumph, but Ros had fallen asleep before Withnail's final speech and Clare had cried alone.

"You look great. I love those jeans on you."

Skinny jeans, a black T-shirt emblazoned with a ragged Iggy Pop barely covering her midriff, cowboy boots, a tattered corduroy jacket, her hair tousled as if glamour had alighted in their parochial community and didn't want to show them up.

"You got home alright?"

"Looks like it."

"Didn't look like it last night." Clare remembered Brian bashing into a table and breaking three glasses. She remembered the bar staff calling time and falling out into the cold night air.

Ros disappeared into the little cloakroom that was always freezing. The dogs looked up from their beds, assuming food. Clare listened to the sound of Ros peeing. She peeled back an edge of cling film and ate a potato. Ros and Scott arguing over who was more over the limit. Ros and Scott ignoring offers of a lift. Ros and Scott saying, *We're fine,* in some sort of unison that made Clare sweat. None of it was fine. Clare felt like she was the only one who could see it coming.

The clank of an ancient flush and Ros reappeared, zipping up her jeans. She leaned in the doorway. "I tried to tell you."

"Tell me what?"

But at that minute, Issy appeared in a pair of Doc Martens, followed by Molly in maroon silk that trailed beads and netting to the floor.

"That's my dress," said Ros.

"Issy stole my boots," said Molly.

"You'll freeze," said Ros.

"You never wear them," said Issy.

"I'm sick of you stealing my things," said Ros and Molly together.

*

The Rectory shone with warmth and light. Freddy ran in; Scott grabbed the cocktail sausages. Tessa had been tasked with a quiche, but the walk into town had defeated her and they'd had to raid the freezer. She watched her husband and son be swallowed by the house, saw Ros flit into view through the kitchen window, Scott reappear holding out the frozen multipack, both of them laugh.

The roar of the party, men in red trousers, their shirts undone one button too many, women in dresses that had looked good in the shop, Diane hurtling about with napkins, Peter pouring wine, the crowd of *amateur-dramateurs* congratulating each other on doing nothing more testing than wearing costumes and forgetting their lines, screeches of *darling* and re-enactments of scenes Tessa couldn't care less about, in-jokes and back-slapping, Freddy had already got bored and gone off to find the teenagers smoking stolen cigarettes in the garden. Tessa had half a mind to follow him. She'd exhausted her *What did you think of the show?* and *What are you doing for Christmas?* and if one more person told her how great Scott was… she pushed her way to the drinks table and held out her glass to Peter.

Three cocktails and half a whisky later, she was more than ready to leave Peter and Diane's lovely sitting room, with its outsize sofas upholstered in cream, its Persian rug that half of Sussex knew Diane had inherited from her grandfather. The fire dancing in the open hearth, the heavy black firedogs growling, no broken lights nor cheap art here, the walls lit softly by Venetian half-chandeliers, an invisible spotlight on an antique woven jacket from Tibet framed in glass, another on the black-and-white photograph of Diane before she'd put on weight and scarves.

Charles, Charles, there it was again, driving her mad, Ros gyrating, draping herself all over him. Tessa watched from the window seat, hidden by the backs of others, the woman who used to be her friend pull Scott up to dance. She'd greeted her as if they still were, as if Tessa's reality was insane. It was crazy-making. It had made Tessa doubt until she'd settled in the window seat to watch. And there it was, the truth while she'd been shut in Mercury Ward, the same old performance, only this time, there'd been no *Tessy, I love you* or *Don't be mad, woman, you're the only one I want.* There'd been silence and anger and *If it happens again, I'm leaving you.*

Barbara bumped through the crowd, but Tessa avoided her eye. She saw Ros and Scott flop onto the sofa, Clare straddle the fat arm beside them, all three chink glasses; how could anyone find her attractive? Clare pretending she wasn't in love, Scott pretending he could have female friends, Ros pretending to have this terrifying life sewn up – the sound of breaking glass brought more screams of laughter and Clare holding aloft the stem of a smashed glass, wine dripping down her wrist. Tessa followed her to the kitchen. The sink was filled with suds, dirty plates piled haphazardly. Tessa dipped her hand looking for a cloth and came up bleeding. Clare looked at the broken wine glass in her hand as if somehow she'd done it.

"Knife," said Tessa; she'd felt the slice one of Peter's carving set chucked in, invisibly. Clare wrapped the broken stem in kitchen roll and gave another to Tessa as Diane swept in, a dustpan of shards held out before her.

"Absolute chaos. And now you?" She saw Tessa's finger. "Plasters in the drawer. Do you need antiseptic?"

Only for Ros, thought Tessa.

She returned to the sitting room. Scott was deep in the sofa, Ros on his knee. She wasn't sure, when she'd reached into the sink again, if she'd only been thinking it was dangerous to leave a knife hidden in suds. When Scott saw her coming, he pushed Ros up as if she was a shield against the point. It wouldn't have met that midriff if he hadn't shoved. But it did.

"What the fuck?" Ros stopped laughing. Her face drained of colour. It was only a moment, a pierce, a pinprick. "Ow." She looked down. They all did. Scott scrambled to his feet.

"Don't fucking touch me." Tessa's hand shook.

The party grew quiet. Everyone watched as a swell of red breached the dam of Ros's fingers and dripped onto the Persian rug. Ros lifted a bloody palm as if to believe it was true. The point of the knife was stained, but only the point. She was lucky it hadn't been Peter's serrated Damascus. The room emptied, coats were put on hurriedly, guests left like rats. Clare came in with Freddy.

"Give it to me." Scott wasn't laughing anymore either.

Ros said, "I think we should tell her."

Tessa said, "Tell me what?"

A piece of cotton wool pressed into her hand by Diane, Ros stood wavering at the sofa. "Scott? We have to tell her. Don't leave it all to me."

Peter gently took the knife from Tessa's hands. Scott

201

patted his pockets, checking for cigarettes, keys. Diane put her hand on Ros's shoulder, but Ros threw it away, lost her balance and from the depths of the sofa said, "We're having an affair. I'm sorry."

"Oh Jesus," said Peter.

"I fucking knew it," cried Tessa.

Clare covered Freddy's ears.

Scott lifted both hands as if to stop traffic. "Tess, I've no fucking idea what she's talking about."

"I fucking knew it," said Tessa again.

"You've no fucking idea?" said Ros.

"Too much to drink," said Scott.

"Was it her that moved the cutlery drawer?" said Tessa and Peter laughed, and Diane told him to shush.

"If you're talking about babysitting Fred, she came round a few times, cooked supper, didn't she, Fred?"

"Don't bring him into it," said Tessa.

"We kissed," said Ros.

Everyone looked at Scott. His mouth moved, but nothing came out of it.

"Did you kiss her?" asked Tessa.

"On stage, I did. On fucking stage. Jesus."

"Scott," Ros tried to get up. "I can't believe you're—"

Scott backed away. "Seriously, Ros, I don't mean to be ungrateful, but there was never any—"

"Any what? Messages? Holding me? Calling me your angel?"

Scott turned to Tessa again. "Seriously, Tess. You've got to believe me."

"I don't have to believe you anything."

"I never touched her."

"You held me," cried Ros.

"On fucking *stage*. Christ, okay, I think we'd better go. Diane, Peter, I'm sorry about this. I thought she was being friendly; it was company, you know? I'd no idea she had all this—"

"Fantasy?" said Peter.

"You're a fucking liar," shouted Ros.

"And you're out of your fucking mind," Scott shouted back.

"Ros," said Peter. "Calm down."

But Ros made it out of the deep pile of cushions and onto her feet. She lurched towards Scott. "You told me there was never a right time to leave." There were tears and there was blood, the cotton wool dropped to the floor. Scott reversed into the fireplace, so she pushed into Tessa instead, her face up close. "He told me it was over; he said he wanted out of his marriage."

Six adults and a child, staring into the ruins of their realities, each believing their reality was true. Nobody moved until Ros put her hands to her face. As she ran from the room, Clare let go of Freddy and ran after her.

27 THE TRUTH ABOUT ROS

More than anything, Tessa wanted to lie down, but Diane said, "Wait," and sent Freddy off to the snug with hot chocolate and Issy. Nancy and Molly must have gone upstairs; they heard a door bang.

"Please take me home." Tessa looked at Peter. He was still holding the knife. He put it down and picked it up again.

Diane pulled them all into the kitchen. "Peter will drive you home. Scott, you can stay here if need be, but I want you both to listen. We have to tell you something," and together, Peter and Diane told Scott and Tessa the truth about Ros.

They sat at the broad kitchen table.

"Tell them about Ben," said Diane.

"Did you know about the funeral?" asked Peter.

"Did she kill someone?" said Tessa. She wouldn't put it past her.

"I remember the first time I met her," said Diane, getting cups from the cupboard, "she said, *Peter was always going to marry my best friend, but you're so much safer.*"

"Nice little backhanded compliment," said Peter.

"They're her specialty," said Diane.

Tessa thought of all the times Ros had said, *Would you like me to help you with your hair?* without prompting. How she'd turn up at her house and say, *Are you okay?* with her head tipped on one side, when Tessa had been feeling perfectly fine until that moment. Ros's specialty was making her friends feel shit, then asking them how they were. She treated her daughters like shopping she regretted; she stole husbands.

Peter said, "It was her best friend's daughter. We never dreamed she wouldn't go. Of course, now we know why."

"They'd met at drama school," said Diane. "Ben was Cara's boyfriend; they were a tight little three. Ros maintained she liked it that way; dependable Cara and Ben while she flitted about having chaotic relationships. She always said she never wanted to get married, didn't want kids, wanted to concentrate on her career, convinced she was going to be the next Vanessa Redgrave. She was always telling us about auditions she was up for, meetings with famous directors that never materialised." The kettle boiled; Diane filled a cafetière.

"When Ben and Cara got married," Peter got the milk out, "something flipped in her, I don't know. Maybe she felt rejected. Maybe she knew things would never be the same. Within a year, she'd married·Harold."

Scott said, "I know about Harold." He rolled a cigarette and played with it unlit, flipping it between his fingers.

"Do you?" said Peter. "Have you met him?"

Ros had always said not to talk about it. She didn't want people to know; they might look down on her, think her weak or pity her. She'd sworn Tessa and Clare to secrecy. *Privacy*, she'd corrected. *I just want to keep it private.*

Tessa took the unlit cigarette from Scott's fingers. "She told me he used to hit her."

Peter said, "Did she now?" and glanced at Diane, who fetched an ashtray from under the sink. "He's the most decent man you'll ever meet."

"Apart from you, my love," added Diane as she disappeared off to the sitting room. She returned with platters of leftovers; tired mini quiches, wrinkled cocktail sausages and a scattering of vol-au-vents.

Scott folded his arms across his chest.

"But she was in a refuge," said Tessa. She couldn't find her lighter.

Diane shook her head. "No, she wasn't."

"She said he almost killed her."

"Christ," said Peter.

"Poor Harold," said Diane.

"Isn't there a restraining order?" said Tessa.

"I think maybe she didn't want to hurt you," said Scott suddenly.

Tessa had avoided looking at him until now. She didn't want to see his sorry face, all Mr Innocent, how was I to know? What a fucking child. He'd walked right into it while she was shuffling about in corridors and crying into stewed tea. Derek and Clive had got Ros's number the moment she'd crouched at Tessa's shoulder – so she'd been on TV, so what? After she'd gone, after Tessa had been dragged back inside, Clive had said, "I watched it a few times, but she only had one way to move her face and that was down. Ethel could knock socks off her," and Ethel had screamed in delight. Derek had said, "There's only two kinds who think they've got it all worked out; psychiatrists, and the ones who march in out of nowhere and five minutes later think they can mend what others have given up as broken, as if gargling aloe vera will solve twenty years of psychosis. It's all for her," and he'd leaned forward out of his chair and taken Tessa's hands, his voice calm. She'd put all her faith in his steadiness. "This fixing, it's only for her to feel better. If I wanted a hero, I'd call Danger Mouse," and Ethel had squealed again.

Scott rolled another cigarette. "Harold's got mental health issues. Is that not right, Peter?"

Peter pinched his nose and blew his cheeks out. "Christ."

"I told you it was a mistake," said Diane.

"We did it for the girls," said Peter.

"Is he not bipolar?" asked Scott.

"He's nothing of the sort," said Peter.

"I don't understand," said Tessa.

"My sister's a fantasist," said Peter and they all looked up as the cuckoo clock struck one.

Scott smoked, Tessa shivered and held out her hand for the lighter. Diane fetched a blanket.

"I don't suppose either of you know where my sister was supposed to be on opening night?"

"On stage, fucking my husband?" said Tessa.

"It was her goddaughter's funeral," said Diane. "She swore she'd told Brian; she begged me not to say anything. She said she didn't want to panic the cast, but I should have known. She said they were going to make an announcement; Elvira would be played by Issy. They wouldn't have to change costumes because they were the same size. I was at South Lodge getting a face peel that Saturday," and her fingers absently touched her own cheek. "As far as I was concerned, Peter had gone off to pick her up. I knew nothing until I walked into the dressing room that afternoon and saw her. She gave me that look, the one she reserves for people who know her. I didn't know what to say. I could hardly have it out there and then, we were up in an hour, I just had to get on and get on stage. But she stayed well away from me that night, I can tell you. Didn't let me near her, not for one minute. All that shrieking and hugging to keep me at bay. I can't tell you what I said when I caught up with her. I was incandescent."

"The point is that Ros didn't go." Peter got the whisky out.

"Is that necessary?" asked Diane.

"Scott likes a drop, don't you, Scott?"

"I'm one big cliché to you, is it?"

"Big soft Irishman," said Peter. "No wonder she went for you."

"I knew it that night at the barbecue," said Diane.

Tessa had known it, too. She'd watched Ros fling herself all over him, but the messages had got confused. The inside hadn't matched the outside. Ros had been her friend. She'd gone on about how Tessa should take the part of Elvira, how she'd *help her*, how she'd *hold her hand*. *You'll be great, Tess. You'll be fine. It'd be good for you. All men need is attention.* Her attention was what she'd meant. Maybe she'd known it would tip Tessa over the edge.

Scott said, "What happened with this Ben?"

"She saw a weak spot," said Diane.

There, thought Tessa.

Peter got a handkerchief out of his pocket and blew his nose. Scott poured himself a whisky. Tessa stubbed out her cigarette and ate another crumbling vol-au-vent.

"Cara had a bit of a blip after she had Poppy."

"Post-natal depression is not a blip," said Diane.

"And Ros stuck her oar in. She used to go on about how Cara wasn't coping, how she was trying to help."

"We said, *Leave them be*, but she couldn't. She was

obsessed with interfering. Then she started telling us that Ben was unhappy, that he kept ringing her."

"It wasn't true."

"I think it was a bit true," said Diane. "She's good at turning herself into an invaluable shoulder to cry on."

"Isn't she just," said Scott.

Later, Tessa would shout, *Take some fucking responsibility,* but not now; now, she was tired.

"We knew something was up." Diane put the kettle on again.

"I took him out for a pint," said Peter. "I warned him. I said, *You want to watch my sister.* But he said there was nothing going on. A difficult patch with Cara, that was all. He said it was great having someone to talk to, someone who knew her as well as he did."

"Then, one day, Cara came home."

"She'd gone to stay with her mother for the weekend."

"And found them in the kitchen with their arms around each other. Ros swore he'd been telling her he was going to leave. He swore he'd been having a bad day and she'd given him a hug, it was nothing, but Cara didn't buy it. She said she'd known something was going on. She accused them of having an affair. Ben denied it. Ros didn't. Cara threw him out. Ros swears to this day that they had."

"Had they?" asked Tessa.

"No," Peter and Diane said together.

"Nothing happened," said Peter.

"Except in your sister's head," finished Diane. "She'd made it up."

"Then why didn't she say so?" asked Scott.

"Because she prefers her fantasy life," said Peter.

Scott looked at Tessa, but Tessa looked down.

"They never spoke to Ros again until last week. They were fine about her going to the funeral. They wanted her to go. It was the past, wasn't it? This bigger terrible thing had happened and they weren't thinking about that other stuff. They thought Ros would want to be there."

"Had they got back together?" asked Tessa.

Peter shook his head. "That's why she came here. When they divorced, she thought Ben would come to her, but, of course, he didn't. He wasn't interested in Ros in that way."

"She was a mess," said Diane. "Harold said it was like living with an actress who hasn't heard the word *cut*. He called it *that acting disease.* He offered her a divorce, but instead she started telling people she was trapped in an abusive marriage and then she said he was touching Issy. That was the end of the line for him. He agreed not to fight for custody as long as she got help. Do you remember when he came over with that book? He said he thought maybe she had a personality disorder."

"She tried saying she was bipolar for a while. It didn't stick. Sorry, Tessa." Peter flattened his hand on the table. "I suppose you'd know better than us. I knew narcissists were self-obsessed, but I didn't know there was all this other stuff."

"It's called magical thinking," said Tessa.

"Well, I don't know about these things, but I do know my sister lives in a world of fabrication. She makes things up; she believes them."

They sat in silence. The clock ticked.

Scott said, "I think I've got to get home."

"I'm not going home with you," said Tessa. She searched her bones for the energy to stand and thought of Freddy, curled in the snug; they'd heard the television being switched

210

off, Issy tramping upstairs. Diane had gone in to look and reported him fast asleep.

Scott carried his son to Peter's car and lay him on the back seat, the blanket over him. Tessa climbed in the front. She wasn't interested in her husband's face; he could stretch out in one of Diane's lovely spare rooms. A victim of a narcissist or a lock and key with a woman who preferred to think that nothing was her fault. Scott was the perfect foil; the opposite to Ros, he brushed over his past as if it was a joke, as if growing up in a war zone was funny. While Ros was probably sniffing glue in biology, he was chucking Molotov cocktails over the playground wall and calling it a laugh. Their fracture lines made sense, denial and exaggeration, anything but the truth. So he'd pitched up in a quaint market town, so he'd found Tessa, the war zones of their childhoods finding an easy match, too; Molotov cocktails replaced by the automatic weapon of her illness, but at least hers was honest. Ros's fed on shame, her disease was a virus that infected, a contagion for which there was no cure. She would lose the sass in her hips, she would turn scrawny, throw herself at the gym and come out looking hard-edged and desperate, and nothing would stop the death of the person she pretended to be, and nothing would halt the rise of the person she was. There was no happiness in her anywhere, only an aching, selfish, panicked insistence to be the centre of everyone's world, to seek out collusion, to take hostage, to punish those who saw through her and, for the first time since their friendship began, Tessa was glad she was nothing like her. For all her loud voice, Ros was a spitfire in tailspin; she was hurtling towards the ground.

Across the lane, the downstairs lights were on at Ros's house, but, as Peter pulled out of his drive, neither of them turned to look.

28   BEING BRAVE

Clare picked up Ros twice on her stumble across the lane.
She'd wasted valuable time locating her bag and coat and
come running out of Peter and Diane's house as Ros lost her
footing and landed on her hands and knees in the dirt.

"He's lying." Ros lurched to her feet, stumbled and fell
forward again.

Clare put her arms around her.

She got her home, she let the dogs out in her search for
tissues – a roll grabbed from the downstairs loo. Crosby and
Nash happy to see them; how were they to know of disaster?
Amid the disarray of shoes kicked off, coats discarded, bags
dropped, they wagged about asking for food and settled,
disappointed, by the Aga. Clare made coffee.

"Bring it upstairs, would you?" Ros wandered away out
of the kitchen leaving soggy, scrunched toilet paper in her
wake, no more blood, just snot and tears. Clare heard the
creak of stairs and checked her phone. No messages from
Tessa. She left it on the counter and found Ros face down on
her bed, cries muffled by her pillow.

The cups of coffee on Ros's bedside table, Clare sat
carefully on the edge of the mattress and stroked her friend's

back as if she were a frightened horse. "It's going to be all right."

"No," Ros screamed and her shoulders shook. "No, no, no." She pummelled the bed like a little girl, her T-shirt rucked, she still had her cowboy boots on. Clare gently eased them off and Ros snaked out of her jeans, the ankles caught on her heels, and she raised her eyes and arms to heaven, let her hands fall limp as if this was the last straw; together, they yanked the denim. Ros took off her T-shirt, too, showing the pinprick stab of blood where Peter's knife had pierced her; already a dried scar, angry, furious, it wouldn't kill her. She touched it and looked at Clare.

"I'm so sorry."

Ros shook her head.

"It isn't like her." A lie. She'd asked Scott more than once, *Why do you stay?* when Tessa, ill and violent, had thrown a bottle at him. *I've got my demons.* He'd stared into his pint. But it had always been on the up, when she was flying, heading for section, not after and on the way down.

Ros stripped off her bra. Clare pretended to look for pyjamas, her hands on an ancient dresser.

"Drawers." Ros's voice was small. "And antiseptic in the bathroom."

Clare took a pair of Calvin Klein yoga pants and a baggy top from the bottom drawer, which took both hands to open.

"And can you get my cigarettes?"

A Dettol wipe from the bathroom cabinet, Ros's jacket on the kitchen floor where she'd dropped it, cigarettes in the top pocket, a bottle of vodka from the freezer, Clare grabbed her own bag as well and slung it over her shoulder. She was sure she had a lighter in there somewhere.

Ros, framed by pillows, pyjamas on, duvet tucked, hair

tangled, mascara smudged, tore the antiseptic wipe open with her teeth, lifted her baggy T-shirt, dabbed at the miniature hole Tessa had made, a brown stain. She tossed it onto the floor and lit her cigarette; a long drag of Marlboro Light and an attempted smile as smoke curled in the air between them, but her mouth crumpled and she started crying again. Clare held out more toilet roll.

Ros waved it away. "Downstairs. Under the sink. It hurts my nose. Sorry." So Clare ran downstairs again and fetched a box of extra-soft Kleenex from among bottles of floor cleaner and spare J-cloths, a pile of plates Ros never used. She flicked off the lights on her way out.

When she got back, Ros had poured them both a shot.

Clare found a spot in the middle of Ros's bed where she could sit cross-legged, but she could still feel Ros's foot hard up against her thigh.

"Can you believe him?" Ros tried to smile again.

"Actually, I can't." She had seen it coming, this electric charge, what straight woman wouldn't be seduced by Scott? How was Ros to know he flirted with everyone, made hay with that voice of his, Tessa his shield from ever having to follow through. Her illness suited him, she'd thought it more than once. Like a man carrying a baby, all the cooing and good looks made trustworthy by a woman at home except his was a position of extra saint; *I don't know how he stays with her* and *Goodness knows she's lucky to have him*. He'd told her Tessa's father had said, *We appreciate you taking her off our hands, old boy, you're a braver man than most*, as if she was a carton of something rotten, a dead weight, not a drop of wonderful about her. Somewhere in that Irish story he loved her, but Sussex had made him soft; he'd sold Tessa for a place with the rugby dads, his voice lost among attitudes of blame, the misunderstanding of human nature. He'd betrayed her long before Ros. Clare took one of Ros's cigarettes. "He's a complete shit."

"Oh no, Clare. Don't say that. He was caught in the headlights. We hadn't planned it." She dropped her head to her hands, "God. Poor Tess. I never meant to hurt her."

"Of course you didn't."

"We got close, you know? Too close. And Tess was away, and he started telling me all these things about their marriage. What was I supposed to do? I thought he was lonely. I mean, it must be so hard. And then one night…"

Clare held her breath.

Ros shook her head as if to shake the memory away. "Afterwards, he told me he was going to leave her."

Clare nodded. "So you did—"

Ros's face crumpled again. Whatever she was going to say was lost in a cloud of smoke.

"I'm sorry," said Clare. "You don't have to talk about it."

"If it hadn't been for the play."

"It's not your fault."

"I should have known he was using me."

"I did try to warn you."

"I thought he was vulnerable."

"It's you who's vulnerable. He took advantage." She looked vulnerable, too, sat there in bed, her skin pale, a protective hand on her belly.

"Everyone thinks I'm so tough." Ros sniffed. "I put on this… persona, you know? Good-time girl? Always a laugh? It's not true."

"I know it's not true."

"I do it for the girls. After what they've been through."

Clare wanted to touch her all over. She wanted to pull off the covers and Calvin Kleins, run her hands down and up those legs, find the old cut where Molly and Issy had been pulled out, the new one where Tessa's knife had gone in, land at the quiet, dark tunnel of her, get inside. She refilled their glasses. "No one's going to believe him."

"But what will I say to Tessa?"

"I'll talk to her."

Ros stretched out her hand and touched Clare's knee. "Would you?"

Clare bit her lip. "She suspected, you know. She kept asking."

Ros put her glass on the bedside table. "Wait." She slipped out of bed and padded from the room. Clare heard her going downstairs. If she stripped off her clothes and slipped into bed, if she was there when Ros returned, what then? She put the vodka on the floor. Ros returned with a book, a credit card, a smile and a small bag clouded with white. "Don't you think?" She put the book flat between them and cut four lines.

Clare leaned on her elbows, a twenty-pound note from her purse held to her right nostril, her left pressed shut while Ros made faces and pinched her nose and shook her head like a horse. The blast made her face feel scrubbed. "Christ."

Ros laughed, did another line, picked up her shot glass and downed it.

Cocaine made the plains change shape and Clare lost track of time and space as line followed shot followed line. She stretched out on the bed, not caring which limbs touched what. Her body was a thing of wonder.

Ros lit a cigarette. "So, when?"

"When what?"

"When did you notice?"

"Notice what?"

"Scott." Ros's voice was plaintive. "And me."

"Oh." For a moment, she'd forgotten. "Lots of times. At the pub, rehearsals, all the time." It felt like all the time. She couldn't remember. Ros was all the time.

"And you think Tessa picked up on something, even before, I mean, before she went in?"

"She's very sensitive." Tessa was her witch friend. She'd have been burnt at the stake.

"Why didn't you tell me?"

Clare refilled their glasses. The effort felt like springing to life from the best of sleeps, as if she didn't want to stop moving ever. She rearranged herself like Ros, cross-legged, the better to be immersed in the bedroom, the bed, the body of this woman she loved, that she wanted to swallow whole. Her cigarette tasted delicious. "I didn't want to get in the middle." Talking was so easy. Her shyness had left her.

"See? She knew. I wasn't making it up. Only I didn't see it till she went away. I mean, I knew he liked me, but I get a lot of attention, you know? I never do anything about it, but it was different with Scott, from the moment I met him, I remember thinking, *Shit*. I tried to keep him at a safe distance, I really did, but it was always there, bubbling under the surface, waiting, and then she left. If she hadn't left, none of it would have happened, I didn't mean it to happen, oh God." She buried her face in her hands again. "Why do I keep falling for it?"

"We all do stupid things. I do stupid things all the time."

"Like what?"

Like love someone like you.

Ros exhaled, sending smoke above Clare's head. "Who was your last relationship? How come you never talk about Nancy's dad? Is he not around?"

"He's in London."

"How come we never see him?"

"He's married. Nancy sees him all the time."

"A married man?"

"No, I mean, he's married now. He's lovely." She thought of Charlie; handsome, sweet Charlie, who'd have dropped everything to be with her.

"Is he safe?"

"Safe?" Clare propped herself up. She'd fallen into a slump, been talking to the ceiling. It was easier than looking at Ros.

Ros touched her again. "You don't have to talk about it."

"No, it's fine. He's lovely."

If she didn't know better, she'd have thought Ros looked disappointed. She held out her glass and Clare nearly fell off the bed reaching for the bottle. When she looked up, Ros was crying again. "Oh, Ros."

"I'm such a fuck-up."

"It's not your fault." She stroked her arm.

"I should have known. How am I going to face anyone?"

"Everyone will understand."

"Maybe I'll go away."

"No, don't."

Ros wiped her nose on her wrist and squeezed Clare's hand. "You're so sweet, Clare. You're so caring."

It was at that moment that Clare felt herself propelled as if by some greater force. She was halfway up Ros's body before she knew what she was doing, her mouth against Ros's lips, her hands in the rough mess of Ros's hair, her chest pressing into her. She was kissing her and touching her and, for a still, beautiful second, Ros was kissing her back, until she wasn't. The violence of her shove threw Clare off the bed.

"What the fuck are you doing?" Ros was shouting, she was wiping her mouth, she was telling Clare to get out. Clare, splayed on the floor, couldn't register what was happening. Her shot glass rolled under the bed. She reached for it as if that was the only mistake of a drunken night.

"Get the fuck out. Get the fuck out of my house."

Clare got to her feet. Somehow, in the moment that had smashed, she'd peeled off her T-shirt. She wrapped her arms around her chest.

"There," Ros shouted, pointing at the floor.

Clare grabbed it and held it to her skin.

"Get out," Ros screamed again.

In her stumble downstairs, she wondered if Nancy and Molly were asleep in the room next door, whether they'd heard anything, but in the kitchen, as the shouting in her head grew quiet, no footsteps followed her, no Nancy wandered in sleepy-eyed asking what the noise was about. She found her phone on the kitchen counter and stared at it. She wondered why it was so hard to figure out where she was, not Ros's kitchen, but which planet. She wanted a coffee but didn't dare turn on the lights, so she stood at the sink in the dark, drinking great gulps of water straight from the tap and threw up half of it.

Get in the car, said her brain. *Get in your car and drive home.* Leave Nancy here who probably wasn't here, who'd probably stayed at Diane's. She looked for her keys. She looked for her bag. She saw it discarded on the floor of Ros's bedroom. For a second, she imagined crawling in, grabbing it, but everything told her that was the cocaine and vodka talking. Her coat, at least, was there where she'd left it when they'd come in and the only drama had been Tessa and Ros; a light stabbing in the Home Counties and a man who'd betrayed them both. Maybe she could walk home. Maybe she could pretend for the hours between now and forever that none of this had happened. That she hadn't launched and ripped and buried her mouth in the smudged red of Ros's lips, that she hadn't believed, for one ecstatic moment, that this was it.

She found her shoes where she'd kicked them off. Crosby and Nash shoving heads beneath her hand, she let them out for a pee. Good, thoughtful Clare, hating herself for her reliability, despising her lack of selfishness. Just once she'd gone out for what she wanted and look where it had got her. She stumbled like Ros, but there was no one there to catch her. She made it to the driver's seat of her bashed-up Subaru that stank of horses and a simple life; she sat there shivering, feeling sick, waiting for something to happen that would change this moment into another moment that moved the whole series of fucking awful moments forward. Her hand on her phone, it lit up the night as she sent a text to the only man stupid enough to not care what she'd done, who'd come and get her no matter the hour. The ringer had broken long ago, so she kept it gripped in her hands. The vibration would wake her.

29   PLAYING CHICKEN

The lights of Brian's truck bumping up the track got Clare out of her Subaru. She waved him to a stop. He leaned across to let her in. His bulk filled the space beside her, cologne and engine oil. She opened her window. A fine mist of wet covered everything; it picked up as they reached the road, spattering the windshield in heavy drops.

"Big night?"

She'd told him she'd lost her bag. He'd texted *can't have gone that far!!!,* the exclamation marks making her head spin. She dreaded the day he discovered emojis.

"I always said she was trouble. Glad our Tessa gave her what for."

Clare had forgotten that bit of the evening, the part where one friend stabbed another.

"I think it was an accident."

"Some accident."

The lights of a food truck came up on their left, a lay-by, an awning and some plastic chairs. Brian indicated. She didn't have the energy to protest the statement or the delay. Sometime between half past one and now, she'd drifted through coma, the vibration of her phone clawing its way up her arm and into her brain enough to rouse her, and as dawn crept over the edge of the golf course, beyond the food truck, Cowdray polo grounds remained bathed in a blackness she wished would last forever. She watched Brian lean against the counter, a farming bulk half the height of the brightly lit figure inside who moved from coffee machine to hotplate, handing over cups and food wrapped in greaseproof paper.

"Breakfast bap." He held out a wrapper.

Clare nearly threw up.

He put hers on the mess between them and handed her a cardboard cup of coffee instead. "Your girl not with you?" Ketchup landed on his shirt as he began the chew and slurp of his own breakfast, a drop of egg yolk followed.

"Peter's giving her a lift." She presumed that's what would happen. School; normal life on a normal Monday in November. The fat watch on his wrist showed a quarter to six. She'd have time to get home, wash and get back to her car before Ros woke up, a spare key kept in the office. "And you're happy to wait? I'll be quick."

His coffee wedged dangerously between his thighs, one hand on the wheel, Clare wasn't sure which was the lesser of two evils, yet the thought of home kept her mouth shut. A few turns of this twisting road, its blind corners and deaf hills, Midhurst to negotiate, but at this hour only farmers ignored the speeding signs, right at the bike shop and up the hill and she'd be able to stick her fingers down her throat, be sick with impunity in her own sloping bathroom, wash away Ros's disgust and her own shame, except she'd never get rid of either completely. Like the words of the girlfriend in Manchester who'd said, *You want to grow up, love,* and called her a tourist, as if her lesbian was a passing fantasy of student life.

There was nowhere in his chaotic truck to put her scalding cup; even with the cardboard slip, the heat burned through to her freezing fingers. The footwell was littered with empty packets of Ginsters sausage rolls, the crinkling yellow of discarded Monster Munch, crushed cans of Red Bull, the story of Brian's diet. A woollen hat and string gloves embedded with straw and mud were stuffed on top of the handbrake, baling twine and pliers rattled entangled on the shelf above the glove compartment; her Subaru looked the same. They both screamed lonely breakfast baps in lay-bys and Clare wanted to open the door and hurl herself onto the speeding road. She took a sip of her coffee through the tiny plastic hole and burnt her tongue.

In Peter and Diane's lovely spare room, Scott was waking up. He couldn't remember what day it was, he couldn't recall why the ceiling was higher than normal, why the sheets felt cleaner or the pillows softer; Diane had offered him a Valium before she went to bed, unnecessary but pleasant, and he'd been out before she'd closed his door, only a passing thought in her head that she'd rather he took off his trousers. He drifted up from the easy depths of Diazepam, familiar to his system since his wife kept a constant supply, turned over and decided to leave the mystery of why the side table didn't look like a broken city of cups gone by, why his alarm wasn't shouting, till later. Surely it was still the weekend. Perhaps Tessa had done some tidying up.

Ros snored, alone in her bed, across the lane.

Nancy, Molly and Issy, who'd all shared a room on the top floor of Peter and Diane's house, scrolled drowsily on Reddit, Instagram and Snapchat, and figured they wouldn't have to get up till seven fifteen earliest.

Freddy crawled into his mother's bed after a nightmare had woken him. He curled against her, while Tessa, glad of the warmth, inhaled the sweet soft of his hair, and dropped again into a heavy sleep.

Brian drew up outside Clare's cottage, the bump of the drive sending coffee over her wrist. She shook it and emptied the cup onto stones and shut the car door with her foot in a single movement that didn't allow for more questions. Horses looked up from their grazing, a rug slipped here, an electric tape sagging there, the to-do list at the stables was never-ending. A few of the girls were already up and mucking out; a couple of owners were chatting by the sand school. Clare hoped they wouldn't grab her. She kept her head down, let herself into the cottage, the door never locked.

Half a tub of water in her sloping bathroom, tepid, she hadn't been there to turn on the immersion. She wished her landlord would put in a shower. Her nostrils clogged and sore, she blew her nose into the water, strands of blood and snot. Brian had shouted, *I'll be right here* as she'd closed the truck door on him; she imagined him imagining her naked – for sure he'd have seen her bathroom light go on. Her head hurt. Her heart hurt. There was no way she could ever go on, but she was absolutely going to have to, because if an alien had watched from a distant planet through a telescope at Clare's last night, they'd have seen vodka and an attempt at a kiss, they'd have seen rejection and white powder smudged on a book and they might have got bored and turned away, offered the view of stupid humans to another because there wasn't much to look at in the greater scheme of things – it was ants fighting on a molehill, it was nothing. A year of nothing love, a year of nothing friendship, twelve months of having everything revolve around a woman called Ros.

Clare dried herself off, the towel scratchy, she'd been out of fabric conditioner for three months, never enough time for anything except watching for her phone to ring, a message to light up her screen: *walk?* or *pub?* And there would be no more. She'd blown it. The last twenty-four hours were the exact reason why Clare kept her mouth shut.

Ros had said to her once, *Such secrets, Clare,* and nudged her with her elbow and as quickly turned her expression to concern, a bottom lip edging forward. *Oh God, I'm sure it's none of my business,* and Clare had let her believe that something terrible lurked in her past, but it didn't, unless shy to the point of painfulness was a beating, in which case Clare was beaten every day. She found clean socks, yesterday's jeans, her knickers turned inside out because she'd forgotten to put on a wash, a T-shirt and sweatshirt stripped off as one, inside out, recovered and put on as one. She didn't dare look at herself in the cracked bathroom mirror. She never wanted to see her own face again.

Day was creeping over the fields as she emerged, a limp effort through the rain, sodden horses and potholes filled with water. She pulled her boots on at the door, grabbed the spare key from the office, her breath made clouds in the freezing air, she gave as little as possible to grim smiles of *morning.* Brian hadn't moved, his thighs splayed either side of the steering wheel as she'd imagined, every piece of his clothing terrified by his size, an ex-soldier turned farmer pleading to be released from moleskin trousers, checked shirt, padded green gilet and tweed cap.

"The trouble with her sort," as if he'd never left off – Clare did up her seat belt – he started the engine, "is that they think they can play men like marionettes, toys to pick up and throw down, like every last damn one of us will bay at her fingertips. Tarting about in her daughter's clothes, tempting men to touch her. I meant to have it out with Scott, warn him, tell him to stay well away. And with Tessa in Spain, I almost got rid of her, you know. I should have. I don't care about *Casualty* this and *Young Vic* that. Actress, my arse. Temptress more like. I'll bet there's a whole heap of skeletons—"

"It wasn't her fault." She didn't want to get into it, only he wouldn't stop talking.

"I would've thought you'd be sticking up for Tessa." He veered round a flooded bit of road, making an oncoming car flash its lights and lean on its horn.

"It wasn't either of their fault."

"You can't blame a man for his dick, if you'll excuse the expression."

Clare couldn't. And she wished he'd slow down.

"And we all heard him say flat-out nothing happened. What that one needs is a firm hand. Put her in her place. If it wasn't for being Peter's sister, I'd have got rid of her completely. Leading him on, leading him a merry dance and all the while Tessa in Spain."

Through Midhurst, over the bridge, the roads flooded and icy. Clare clung on to the door, the better to avoid being flung into Brian as he took another corner at speed.

"I've a good mind to go over there myself, tell her what for, that dinner party, do you remember? As if I didn't know I wasn't invited. If I hadn't bumped into her at the farm shop, I'd never have known. What am I? Not good enough for Little Miss from London? She probably wanted Scott all to herself."

And yet she'd let her think he'd followed her there. Clare tried to remember. If only her mind would de-fog.

"I'd say Scott's had a close shave."

"For fuck's sake, Brian, Scott's done what all men do." She didn't mean to shout, but the truck was so loud and the rain hammered down and the sky was so angry, so thunderous she thought it might bolt lightning at them, end it for them both, a storybook conclusion, everyone would say, *I always thought they should be together, isn't it sad?*

"Now, Clare," began Brian, but Clare cut him off.

"Tessa wasn't in Spain. Okay? She was in hospital. She was sectioned; she didn't want people to know. And Ros didn't do anything – she was trying to help. Did you know her ex used to beat her up? Did you know she was in a refuge? She moved here to get away from him. Why would she throw all that up for a made-up affair with her new friend's husband? It's him you want to have a go at. He's totally fucked her over and Tess, and he doesn't give two shits about it, he doesn't even have the balls to admit it. She's devastated. We all are."

Clare pictured Ros, her head on the pillows, so animated, so vulnerable and the screaming horror that replaced what Clare had thought she loved. But that wasn't love, to launch yourself at someone, that wasn't care. The mountain of Ros's friendship loomed large, blocking out the view, and Clare found herself at the bottom, bruised and cut – a night that had ruined everyone.

"She'll probably have to leave. She's my friend and I'm going to lose her, she's going to go away, I'll probably never see her again, and fuck knows what Tess is going to do. Six weeks in Mercury Ward and she comes out to that. He's a fucking arsehole."

It was a rule, to never cry in front of Brian, but at about the time they reached the main road, the straight shoot from Midhurst to Petworth that wasn't straight at all, which twisted and turned through a sodden Sussex morning, ice and slush and wet leaves, that rule was broken. She'd started crying around *he's totally fucked her over* and by the time *I'll probably never see her again* was choked out, she was wiping the back of her hand across her face.

"He's hurt you."

"He hasn't hurt me."

"He's hurt your friend."

"He's fucked with everyone I love." And this made her cry harder, saying it out loud, to Brian, of all people, who knew he'd be the one to hear it, but Brian was driving too fast, his hands tight on the wheel, his lips muttering something that Clare couldn't hear. *A man can't walk out on his wife just because she's not well* was lost in the shortness of his breath.

Scott, at the wheel of his Land Rover, changed gear to speed up the hill away from Peter and Diane's lovely home. He'd woken with a jolt of remembering. He'd showered and put on the same clothes, drunk a cup of last night's coffee reheated, found his keys and bumped down the drive. The girls had been milling about the kitchen, Peter had appeared looking groggy, there'd been murmurs of toast and not missing the bus. Issy had complained about the rain. None of this was Scott's business; he wanted to get home, he wanted to find Tessa, he wanted to find a way to say sorry. The road rose and fell and rose again. He saw a flash of headlights, a car coming towards him, a truck overtaking. He slowed in case it hadn't seen him. The next brow was blind. He'd seen accidents there before.

In the cab of Brian's truck, Clare was screaming. She tried to grab the wheel, but Brian pushed her off. They'd seen Scott's Land Rover approaching, the black-and-white stripes zipping through the storm towards them, unmissable. Brian wouldn't pull back into his lane. He was holding her away with one arm, he was shouting, "Don't worry now, Clare, we just want to scare him. A man can't go walking out on his wife just because she's got problems in the head," but the rain obliterated their view and the storm made them deaf, and a blind hill got in their way, and a zebra ran into the forest, wheels spinning, and was lost among trees.

PSYCHOSIS IN THE
HOME COUNTIES

Mental illness, that catch-all, hadn't caught what they'd feared
would put them outside the close-knit cosiness of country
life, the dinner parties and barbecues, the invitations to join
in. Smashing up the kitchen and lying in the pond were a
punishable offence, yet make everyone in the room feel
lacking, tragic, frightened and you'd be rewarded; a man could
be made president for that, a woman could ride roughshod.
Why the collusion? Why was narcissism treated with mirth,
a quick eye roll, its viciousness allowed? Ros had caused as
much harm if not more, been as destructive yet had been left
to roam free, whereas Tessa, trussed and dribbling for her
confession, had been locked in Mercury Ward, sectioned for
being the shadow they'd rather not see, the easy target, the
one everyone could agree on. Perhaps, Tessa thought, as she
drove from Midhurst to St Richard's, Freddy beside her, if
she'd been pretty or blonde, or loud or sort of famous, if she'd
been as exciting as Ros, they'd have rushed to her defence,
too. They'd have said, *You know Tessa, its DIY! And she likes
swimming with her clothes on,* and had a good laugh about it
and turned a blind eye to her act outs, the way she expressed

the madness inside. Maybe if she'd been the life and soul and as good a liar, she'd have been celebrated for being awful and she'd have got over it, fixed up the kitchen, dried her clothes and no one's marriage would have been wrecked, no one's heart or spine broken. Narcissists gave people permission to act badly, while bipolar psychotics made everyone else feel well. We are all responsible for making one thing okay and not another.

The blossom was out, the air was warming up, winter coats were not quite put away. The weather could turn cold again. Tessa and Freddy kept theirs on as they made their way across the car park to the hospital; Mercury Ward a rooftop through the trees, Tessa focused her sights on the main entrance to St Richard's and held her son's hand across the road. Scott had survived the crash, but only just. He'd been catapulted through the windshield, narrowly missing the trunk of a Douglas fir, and stopped in his tracks by the lowest branches of a beech that he'd hit neck first. His days of climbing oaks, a chainsaw strapped to his chest, a hard hat on his messy Irish head, were over; there would be no more tree surgery for him, only months and months of surgery on his spinal column until he was ready to go home. Which was today.

When the police had knocked on Tessa's door, three months earlier, the day of the crash, when they'd taken off their hats and asked if they might come in, she'd been sure the psychosis had returned. She'd seen flashes of a zebra, wheels spinning; she'd tried to keep it together. She'd sent Freddy to his room, but he was wise enough to know that police meant something bad. He'd seen them at his house before. She rang Clare, but Clare didn't answer. She rang Diane, who came over to sit with Freddy, while Tessa, driven in the back of the panda car, was taken to A&E. The police told her he was breathing. Staggered at her kitchen table the following day, she heard the crunch of wheels outside and went to look. Clare's Subaru. Clare getting out and slamming the driver's door. She looked terrible. When Tessa let her in, Clare hugged her and started to cry.

She watched hopelessly, her friend trying to gather herself, find tissues, take off her coat; her sleeve caught on a button and she swore, ripped it off, and dropped her Barbour inside out on the floor. Her terrier, nervous, jumped at her feet and cocked a leg on the boot rack, peeing directly into Freddy's welly, so the first five minutes were spent getting cloths and saying *It doesn't matter.* By the time they faced each other in the quiet of Tessa's kitchen, Clare was crying again.

Tessa said, "The doctor says he hasn't punctured anything, so…" The kettle hissed. Out of the cupboard with the crack up the side, she got two cups. "They don't know what happened. He veered off the road. They think there must have been someone else involved; there are tyre marks, apparently. They've put out signs for witnesses." A carton of Cowdray half-fat organic milk from the fridge. Tessa imagined the yellow signs, handwritten *Did you see?* in magic marker being sprayed by passing cars on the road out of Midhurst. She put two cups of instant coffee on the table.

Clare said quietly, "Brian's gone to the police."

It took all morning to get the story clear, for Clare to explain and re-explain, and go over it until the fragments made sense. Clare crying, Tessa crying, Tessa angry and Clare distraught.

"It was all lies," said Tessa. She tried to roll a cigarette. It kept going everywhere. And after Clare listened and nodded and fought and argued and dropped her face onto her folded hands, Tessa said, "Have you seen her?" But Clare shook her head.

The whole of West Sussex heard a few days later that Brian had been arrested for dangerous driving with intent to cause harm. It was reported in the *West Sussex Gazette* along with his old discharge report from the army, which outlined a case of PTSD following back-to-back tours in Iraq. The farm shop was abuzz with it. They'd have to find someone else to supply their beef.

But the blossom was flowering and Scott was coming home, not home to Tessa but home to a rented flat in Horsham – a ground-floor one-bed apartment, an insurance payout, and a pull-out bed for Freddy, no stairs, a galley kitchen, a yard of dirty cigarette butts he'd have to clean when he could figure out how to walk. He would walk again, but not into Tessa's life. Three months of coping alone had reminded her that she could cope. Scott had cared and loved her, but her illness had become a marker between them, a difference that said she was ill and he was well and he was a saint for sticking by her. She'd forgotten that she'd managed before, that she'd had years without him; she had more power to her elbow than either of them had believed. She couldn't cook and she was a terrible cleaner, but she knew how to organise her life, all be it in a smaller house; their home with the broken kitchen cupboard, the walls that had shut her in, no island, a pond in the garden was for sale. She was looking at places in Brighton. Their divorce would take another year.

He smiled when he saw them and held out his arms to Freddy, who hugged him and passed him his crutches. He hadn't fought when she'd said, *It's over*; he'd said, *We gave it a shot*, in that typically Irish way that ignored the mountain of pain before them, that made a joke of it. He shut the door on his feelings like a good Belfast boy for whom war was a game and fear an annoyance to be ignored in case it swamped him, in case it stopped him from talking completely. Though he said *Nothing happened* about a hundred times more, what had happened was a breach of trust. It was him who'd been the one she relied on to not throw her to the lions, discuss her in the sunshine of competitive picnics in the polo grounds, hampers and plastic glasses; another marriage wrecked on the shores of Chardonnay. Home Counties hypocrisy had got him; he'd fallen for it. She wouldn't be surprised to see him in red trousers and checked shirt, an amusing belt to demonstrate he hadn't lost his touch. He wasn't Scott anymore and he'd said *Fuck off* when she'd shouted it, in a tone that meant he was ashamed.

She slung his bag over her shoulder. Freddy gathered get-well cards from the windowsill and laughed as his dad got the striding wrong and bumped into the door. He'd been taken to see him every Saturday, but home hadn't been the same without him. Like when his mum wasn't there, a dad-shaped hole like the mum-shaped one when she went away. Nobody thought he noticed. He knew she had an illness, that she threw things and couldn't make supper and cried or worse, stood still for hours, staring at the garden, but she was his mum, the only one he had. Tessa had explained Scott would have a new home now and he'd wondered if it was because of him.

Across the car park and into the car, nurses thanked along the way, Freddy in the front, Scott behind with his leg stretched out. Crumbs from crisps and pieces of Lego knocked off the seat. He would spend between now and the summer falling over and getting up, getting frustrated, angry, looking at the past, thinking how it could have been different, how he could have done it better, whether his injuries would stop him from retraining as a gardener, if Tessa would forgive him, if he would forgive himself. He would love her and try to get her back. She would refuse.

But for Brian, the future was different. It only takes a few tweaks – less money, a different job, fewer friends, an accident borne of pain that has no outlet – for a man just coping to become one who does not. In the small hours of the morning that Scott came out of hospital, Brian balanced on the cab of his tractor to tie a knot, the barn dark and dusty, an owl had flown out as he'd gone in. Straw and mouse droppings showered his eyes, covering his face in a blanket of farming as he slid it along the rafter so that his feet wouldn't reach. The police would later wonder why he was so covered in dirt. Poor Brian. No one had taken much notice of him at all. The news didn't filter down for a week; it took three days for anybody to realise he was missing. He didn't get the help he needed; the training to not speak of his feelings got him flinging a rope as if it was a question of polarity, to be here or not, a simple yes or no. When news got out, the people of Midhurst greeted it with a mixture of guilt and sorrow. Tessa understood. Clare remembered him with horror. Diane and Peter wished they'd known. Only Barbara cried. Ros didn't care. She was too busy packing.

Tessa didn't know Ros had left until she went round to Diane's and Peter's and heard Molly ask if it was okay to use picture hooks in her room.

"Just be precise with the hammer, darling," replied Diane, casting a quick glance at Tessa.

"Is Molly living here?" said Tessa.

"Oh," Diane slid a casserole out of the bottom oven, "they're both with us."

"Mum's gone to LA," said Molly, coming in with a toolbox. She put it on the table.

"For a while," added Diane.

And that was that. Ros's illness, if Tessa cared to think about it, was born of trauma, too; a different set of events, an identical fine mist of denial, a perfect front, a darkness behind which lurked things unspeakable, but she didn't – care to think, that is. She had her own peace to make and she wasn't the one taking hostages, human shields to the demons inside. Tessa had room for herself, her son, the friends who didn't judge her or hurt her or make her feel shit. Ros would have to fight her battles alone, which she did with a new set of friends and a new set of lies and the freewheeling confidence that a British accent brought in Santa Monica. It lasted a year.

Tessa's recovery was slow and messy, but such is the way of it; shiny surfaces and steam-cleaned pelmets, a family dog click-clacking on a scrubbed kitchen floor were never the truth. She had good days, she had bad, she had times when she wanted to give up and others where she knew that wasn't an option. She didn't want to end up like Ethel. With the help of Dr Stemping, she tried to get her meds right, and with the help of a psychotherapist, she returned to the cupboard in her mind, the trauma in her body, the fine mist of abuse that can make a child mad, the assault on her senses that had haunted her. She learnt that her parents had been lying. She learnt how to manage her illness. She took a bit of exercise and mostly ate better, she practised techniques to calm and soothe, be nicer to her frightened self, treat it with the same quiet love she gave her son. If she carried on like that, then maybe there was a chance of not falling so catastrophically that only the arms of Mercury Ward would catch her. Manic episodes were not over, but they were managed; to Clare and Diane, the friends with whom she agreed the white flag, she said, *Raise it if you think I'm losing it*, and they did, and she got help, and they took care of Freddy. She would always be susceptible to exaggerated highs and death-defying lows, her vulnerabilities remained the same, but with a scaffold of friends and professionals, a faith that she rebuilt brick by brick, she developed the language of help all over again, mended it from when it was broken, when she'd fallen out of a cupboard, asked for comfort and been met with tinkling laughs and false smiles, the shine of ice, gin and tonics sparkling in the sunshine, her sisters playing skip rope on the lawn.

ACKNOWLEDGEMENTS

This novel is, and always has been, a love letter to my impossible friend. It's her I thank first and foremost for letting me tell it, for surviving, for being the brave, brilliant, annoying, complex person she is.

For Scott, my thanks to Gillian Dove, and for further research into medication and the mental health system, Clare Griffin. Credit to David Paich, and thanks, for the use of those Africa lyrics. Equally my thanks to ABR for Noël Coward permissions.

Thank you to my agent, Jenny Savill, who believes in me. Your unerring support is gold. To Andrew Wille, who believed in this novel from the start, and whose early feedback and editing felt like proof I had something. I wish for every writer to have a cheerleader like you.

To all those on Substack, you know who you are, who tuned in every week to read the next instalment as it was serialised, you gave me the confidence and encouragement I needed to bring it to life. And to all those readers since who've put up their hand for review copies, the book clubs and bloggers, thank you. Readers are everything, and every reader counts.

To Andy, Blake and Jacobi, I always say this, and I'll say it again, pity the family of a writer. I am absent much of the time, but without you this dance would be lonelier. You are my world.